CHRISTMAS CAPTIVE

JUDAH KNIGHT

Christmas Captive
by Judah Knight

Cover Art Credits:
- Photo 23269943 / Beautiful © Chaoss | Dreamstime.com
- Photo 31920837 / Beautiful © Andreykuzmin | Dreamstime.com
- Photo 471947534 by Lorado – istockphoto.com
- Photo 156423596 by Tomwachs – istockphoto.com

Printed in the United States of America
ISBN-13: 978-1-944483-45-6

Follow Judah Knight through the following media links:
Website/blog: www.judahknight.com
Twitter: @judahknight

Greentree Publishers: www.greentreepublishers.com

CONTENTS

Special Gift Offer

Thank you for choosing *Christmas Captive,* a stand-alone book in the Davenport Series. Whether you've read the previous six books in the series or not, you will be able to enjoy this novella. If you haven't read the other books in the series, we invite you to order them today:

- *The Long Way Home*
- *Hope for Tomorrow*
- Finding My Way
- *Ready to Love Again*
- *Love Waits*
- *No Greater Love*

We offer descriptions of these books at the end of *Christmas Captive,* or you may want to visit Judah Knight's website at judahknight.com.

Special Request:

We would like to ask for a favor. Will you go to your retailer and write a review? Your review will be such a help for someone looking for a clean, romantic-suspense book. Writing reviews are simple. Choose a star ranking, click the appropriate number of stars, and jot down a sentence or two describing your thoughts about the book. Thank you.

Offer:

 As a way of saying thanks for your interest in Judah Knight's *Davenport Series*, we are offering you a gift. Request a free copy of his novella entitled *A Girl Can Always Hope* by visiting judahknight.com/free-gift. In *The Long Way Home* (Book 1), you learn the two main characters knew one another as teenagers. Margaret Robertson (Meg Freeman in *The Long Way Home*) had a crush on her brother's best friend, Jon Davenport. Read the fun, short story of one awkward middle schooler's attempt to capture the impossible catch. We will send you a free copy in a pdf format.

Now, we hope you enjoy the *Christmas Captive*.

GreenTree Publishers

Chapter One

Kate Walker stood in the wide hallway and eased the massive, oak bedroom door closed. Her heart pounded so loudly she thought she'd awaken the whole family. The last thing she wanted to do was alert her parents she was leaving. She'd managed to convince them at dinner she was tired and wanted to go to bed early. The other option would have been to sit in the living room and listen to Grandma Gina tell stories about when Mom and Aunt Julie were kids. Kate had heard enough of those stories to last a lifetime.

She didn't know if her parents had gone to bed or were still sitting up talking. She assumed bed. Either way, Kate knew if she didn't leave now, she'd never meet Brad at McClanahan's. She'd never been to the bar, but Brad said it was a happening place, and that's all she needed to know. She stared down the long hall and saw the light was out. *They're in bed.*

Kate pulled out her phone to check the time—10:05. When she met Brad at the mall earlier that day, he told her when he'd be arriving at McClanahan's. All she had to do was convince what's-his-face at the main entrance she had to return to school. Her visit with good ol' Grandma had to be short. Would he believe she had final exams a week before Christmas? Maybe she'd better say she had to return to Charlottesville for work. That reason would be more convincing.

Her mind went back to her chance meeting with Brad. What a hot guy! He said he was a senior at Georgetown. Right. And she was Chelsey Weimar. Whether he attended Georgetown wasn't important. He was gorgeous, and that's all that mattered.

Although she passed several of the nightshift personnel while en route to the main exit, she made it to the outside entrance without incidence. The first guy she passed gave her the once over, causing her stomach to flip. He was cute, but she had a date with Brad. She'd smiled and told the young…whatever he was…she had to get back home. He bought the lie. Men were easy.

The guy with her car keys was a different story. "You sure are headed out late, Ma'am."

Ma'am? How old does he think I am? Kate cleared her throat. "Uh, yeah, well, I've got to get back to Charlottesville. I've got to work tomorrow. I'm Kate Walker. The red Toyota is mine."

"Charlottesville? University of Virginia?"

"Yep. I'm a senior." *He doesn't have to know I'm a sophomore.*

He had wanted to call Grandma Gina, but Kate insisted he not do that. She told him her grandmother had gone to bed, which was the reason Kate was just now leaving for the two-hour drive back to Charlottesville. She didn't know what lie she'd tell when she returned in a few hours.

He drove up in her Toyota ten minutes later. She saw him typing something into a computer which she assumed was her name and time of departure. Hopefully, her mother would never learn she'd left the place before 10:30.

Her mother was probably lying in bed worrying over any of the 127 things she always worried over. Kate knew she was probably number one on her mother's list. She'd be back in her bed long before her mother knew she'd left.

Once past the bouncer at McClanahan's, Kate walked straight to the bar. Her fake I.D. worked every time. She had decided on the drive over it would be better for Brad to spot her instead of the other way around. Her plan worked.

She felt his hands on her bare shoulders before he spoke. "Hello, gorgeous."

Kate turned and found herself staring into the beautiful green eyes of her new heartthrob. She was so glad she'd worn the over-the-shoulder top. She knew it showed just enough skin and hoped it would drive Brad crazy.

"Hey, Brad. I told you I'd come."

She took his hands and stood from the stool. She pressed her body against his and surprised him with a brief kiss.

He smiled down at her and kissed her again. "Well, Kate. Glad you could make it. You look amazing."

Brad took her by the hand and led her to a corner table. He slid into the booth beside her and ordered drinks before pulling her into his arms.

The night couldn't have been more perfect. They danced, drank, and made out in the booth. She lost count of how many beers she'd downed. Kate knew she'd better be careful. The last thing she wanted was to be pulled over for drunk driving.

She didn't want to admit it, but she felt smashed. She tried to read the blurry numbers on her phone but couldn't make out the time. Didn't matter. She needed to get back. Maybe she and Brad could get together tomorrow. What she needed now was the restroom.

Kate pressed her lips against Brad's again and wrapped her arms around his neck. She bit his earlobe before whispering, "I've got to go to the restroom." She bit him again and giggled.

Kate couldn't walk a straight line. All she knew was she'd better get to the restroom fast. Head spinning, she finally shoved open the restroom stall door. Kate knew she wouldn't be able to drive home for a while. *Looks like I get to spend some more time with Brad the Beautiful.*

When she stepped to the sink, she thought she might throw up. She took in a few deep breaths and rinsed out her mouth. As she braced herself on the side of the sink with both hands, the room began to spin and the faucets on the sink started moving back and forth.

Kate felt a sting. *What was that?* She reached back but felt nothing unusual. Had she heard something? She wondered if she had imagined it. *I've got to lay off the booze.* She looked in the mirror, but everything was out of focus. Her knees felt weak.

Kate leaned against the wall and slid to the floor. She felt hot. *How much did I drink?* Beads of sweat popped out on her forehead. She looked up at the light before everything went black.

Chapter Two

Jon Davenport merged onto Interstate 66 and began heading east toward downtown Washington, DC. Looking at Meg, he felt warmth fill his heart. *What a fortunate man I am.* She turned her head, smiled at him, and leaned over to kiss his cheek.

"I think every day how blessed I am to have you as my wife." Jon squeezed Meg's hand before focusing on the road again.

"Oh, Jon. I'm the one who's blessed. After everything we've been through the last three years, I'm reminded every day is a gift."

"So true." Jon winked at her.

Thoughts of the boys they'd been able to help through their summer program filled his mind. The boys had been a blessing. Just giving them a chance to get off the streets and pursue a different kind of life brought Jon and Meg satisfaction.

They'd found their share of treasure over the last years. Whether they ever found another gold coin wouldn't matter as long as they could rescue boys from the inner-city nightmare.

Probably the biggest blessing of last summer was seeing the transformation in their niece, Lacy.

He had no doubt that their other intern, Kerrick Daniels, would soon be joining their family. He half expected Kerrick to propose to Lacy when they came to Washington in a few days. Lacy was still so young, but she'd grown up a lot over the summer.

Interrupting his thoughts, Meg said, "Judy sure was sweet to take care of Carla for a few days so we could travel up here together. I already miss our little cherub."

"She didn't sound like a cherub when you placed her into Judy's arms. Carla may think of Judy as her grandma, but Judy's no replacement for her mama."

Meg grimaced. "It broke my heart to leave her, but we need some time alone."

Jon squeezed her hand again. "They'll be up here in time for Christmas. Christmas at the White House! Would you have ever thought you'd be spending Christmas with the president of the United States?"

Meg laughed and leaned back on the headrest. "I've got to confess that until I met you, there were a lot of things I couldn't imagine. Now, they're almost commonplace."

"I'm going to take that as a good thing."

"Most of them are. I could do without a few of our experiences over the past three years."

"Come on," Jon teased. "You know you've loved every minute of it."

"Don't know about that, but I'm pretty excited about coming back to Washington. I'll never get tired of going to the White House. I can't believe we're actually here."

"Randall told us to come back to the White House for Christmas. When the President of the United States tells you to do something, you're supposed to do it."

Meg laughed. "Which has more power? The President inviting you over for Christmas or your father-in-law? I suppose he's both, sort of."

Jon smiled. How can someone sort of be the President's son-in-law? Even though Julie had been dead for five years and he was no longer related to Randall Johnson, the President still treated him like family. And he and Gina had taken to Meg as if she were their real daughter.

"If Randall's my father-in-law, that makes you the President's daughter," Jon quipped. "After all, he walked you down the aisle at our wedding."

"He's one amazing man. If Julie was anything like him or Gina, she was a wonderful woman. He really does treat us like family—I mean blood family. I don't understand it."

"It's because he loves us and always will."

Reaching out for the dash, Meg gasped, "Look out, Jon, he's going to hit us!"

Jon grabbed the steering wheel with both hands and slammed on the breaks as a dark SUV flew by and swerved in front of them, barely missing the front of their car. Jon saw the tinted windows and recognized the government tag on the back.

"Politician," Jon muttered, his heart racing. "They think they own this town, and the laws mean nothing to them."

"Even though they make the laws," Meg said with her hand on her chest. "I thought we were going to wreck."

"What is it with politicians and lawyers? They can be so arrogant."

"That's not fair, Jon. We know some politicians and some lawyers who are outstanding people. Randall is a politician."

Jon laughed. "True. Generalizations always get me into trouble."

"Speaking of lawyers, did Jennifer and Michael work it out to join us for Christmas?" Meg asked.

Jon loved Jennifer, Julie's sister, but she was nothing like his first wife. Her husband, Michael, was hard to get to know, too. Jennifer apologized so often it nearly drove Jon crazy. It seemed that in her mind, Julie had been perfect in every way. Jennifer viewed herself as the total opposite of her younger sister, and now that Julie was gone, Jennifer had dug her own hole of self-defeat even deeper.

"Yep. They got here late yesterday, and shock of all shocks, Kate is with them."

"I'm really concerned about her, Jon. I mean Kate. What is she? Nineteen or twenty? So many issues. Jennifer confessed to me a few months ago that Kate had an abortion, and it wasn't her first one. I want to help her, but I'm not sure how."

"The whole thing's a cycle," Jon said, gripping the steering wheel harder. "If Jennifer would get over herself and if Michael would act like he loved his family, Kate wouldn't be trying to get the attention of every guy she passes."

Meg reached over and rubbed Jon's arm. "Jon, you can't always get angry every time we talk about Jennifer and Michael."

"I'm not angry." Jon's jaw tightened as his voice raised a little. "And I don't get angry every time we talk about them."

Meg looked at him and smiled. "Could have fooled me."

Jon stared into the traffic. Kate had problems, but it didn't have to be that way. "I'm sorry, Honey. You're right. I am angry. I know I blame Jennifer and Michael for Kate's struggles. I've got to work on that problem. I mean work on me."

Meg patted his arm and looked back out her window. "When I think of Kate, my heart breaks. With every abortion, there are at least two victims, and she's going to struggle with these decisions eventually."

Jon pulled Meg's hand to his mouth and kissed it. "If there's anyone in the world who can help a troubled girl, it's you, Meg. She's fortunate to have you as her aunt."

"So, I'm her aunt now?"

Jon grinned. "Close enough."

He guided the rental car through the first gate leading to the White House and began the rigorous process of satisfying the Secret Service so they would be allowed into the President's quarters.

He looked up to see the snipers on the roof and the barricades blocking people from driving in front of the structure. He remembered hearing his father talk about taking a tour of the White House when he was a boy. How times had changed! Within fifteen minutes, they stepped into the elevator that would take them upstairs to the president's private quarters.

"Jon and Meg!" Gina cried out as the Davenports stepped off the elevator. "I'm so glad you were able to come. Where's Carla?"

Jon and Meg took turns hugging Gina.

"Judy wanted to keep her for a few days," Meg said. "They're coming up Friday with Lacy and Kerrick. She insisted Jon and I have some time alone."

"I can't wait to see her, and I look forward to catching up with Lacy and Kerrick. Young love and all that. And Judy! Such a sweet and wise woman. I suppose she's more like family than a housekeeper."

"She's family, all right," Jon agreed. "And as far as Lacy and Kerrick are concerned, I have no doubt we'll be planning a wedding within the next year."

"How exciting," Gina said. "In the meantime, you both need to unwind and relax. We want your time here to be stress free and replenishing. You hear that, Dr. Davenport? Replenishing. Read a good book, take naps, love your sweet wife, and eat some wonderful food."

Jon laughed. "Loving my wife is definitely on the menu. I don't know about naps. You know I'm not a nap kind of guy. Where are Jennifer and Michael?"

"I'm not sure. They said they needed to step out somewhere. They'll be back after a while. I'm sorry Randall won't be here until Friday."

"Someone's got to run the country," Jon said. "Hopefully his meetings in Europe will prove fruitful."

Gina looked up and nodded to someone down the hall. "You ready for lunch? I've asked the kitchen staff to wait until you arrived to serve us, and they're ready."

"Kitchen staff?" Meg chuckled. "I could get used to this."

"The truth is I cook as much as I can," Gina said. "I miss doing the simple things of life."

"I must confess Judy does a lot of the cooking at our house," Meg said. "I'm spoiled too, and I don't miss cooking at all. Trust me. It's not one of life's simple things to me. I don't think Jon misses my cooking either."

Jon started walking toward the dining area. "I think I'll stay out of this conversation. Anything I say may hinder one of the goals of this trip." He winked at Meg.

Gina laughed as she and Meg followed. "The presidential doghouse is currently occupied by our cocker-spaniel, so I suggest you be on your best behavior."

Chapter Three

Charles Fields took the final turn before his office parking lot faster than normal, causing his tires to squeal. He knew he'd better calm down or someone might wonder why he was driving instead of his normal driver. He screeched to a halt in his parking spot.

Slamming the door to the dark SUV, he spit out a curse. *I should fire the whole lot of them.* Of course, he knew if he fired them, he'd have to kill them. The way he felt this morning, killing the idiots would be a pleasure.

Their tardiness had caused him to miss his Foreign Relations Subcommittee meeting that morning. Now, he'd have to make up an excuse that could be verified if some nosy reporter chose to investigate.

He owed a lot to the Foreign Relations Subcommittee that no one would ever know about. His participation years ago on the subcommittee for South Asia and Counterterrorism provided him the opportunity to begin his little side business that so far had netted him millions of tax-free dollars.

He paused with his hand on the door to his office building and tried to compose himself. The rule was he always had first dibs with the new talent, and his retrievers had royally screwed this one up. The new girl was beautiful. Drop dead gorgeous in fact. They'd nearly killed her with a drug overdose the night before, and he didn't dare touch her yet. The last thing he needed was to be implicated in the death of some runaway. Of course, she probably wasn't exactly a runaway.

It wouldn't have been the first girl they'd lost, but he didn't have time to deal with the headache of getting rid of a body right now. He'd been up all night waiting on her arrival, only to learn this morning she might not even live through the day.

Right now, he had important business that needed his focus. He'd call Reggie after a while to make sure the girl was still alive. If she came out of it by tonight, he'd have his reward when he returned home. If she treated him well, he might even keep her a few days before sending her to the auction. He didn't fully understand the dark web, but he owed the technology a lot.

"Good morning, Senator Fields," the gorgeous blonde said as Charles stepped out of the elevator onto the third floor.

Charles eyed the young woman standing in front of him, and for the life of him he couldn't remember her name. He did, however, remember her face. His eyes roamed down her slender neck to her name tag. "Good morning, Ginger. You look nice today." *Be careful, Charles. She may get you for sexual harassment. You don't need that.*

Ginger's face glowed as she looked down for a moment. "Thank you, Sir. I'd wondered..."

"Please, Ginger. Call me Charles. You wondered what?"

Her cheeks glowed. "Oh, nothing. It's just good to see you this morning. Mrs. Sanderfield wanted me to meet you at the elevator and hand you these files."

I'd much rather look at you than old Maddie Sanderfield. "Thank you, Ginger." He reached out his hand to take the files and allowed his hand to rest on hers. He lingered for an extra moment before taking the files. His pulse quickened as he looked into her blue eyes.

"You're welcome, Senator, uh, Charles. Uh, Mrs. Sanderfield also wanted me to tell you you're supposed to be across the street in five minutes. You're scheduled to meet with some lobbyist about...I'm sorry, Senator, uh, Charles, I can't remember. Something to do with the pipeline."

"Ok, thank you, Ginger. You've been helpful. Maybe we can get together later. I'd like to hear about your aspirations. Maybe I can help you move up a little."

"Oh, Charles. I'd like that very much."

Charles turned and pressed the button to call the elevator. Fortunately, it hadn't gone anywhere, and the door opened. He looked at his watch and saw he had four minutes to get across the street. He'd have to check in with Reggie after his meeting.

Two hours later, Charles wormed his way through the crowd at the Union Pub and aimed for outdoor seating. He needed privacy and spotted several available tables. Once seated, he reached for his cell phone about the time a reporter pulled up a chair and leaned on his elbows.

"So, Senator Fields. Why did you miss the Counterterrorism Subcommittee meeting this morning? You don't think terrorism is a problem in our world?"

Charles slipped the phone back into his pocket. "Mr. uh, let's see, Robertson, is it?" Charles knew the fool's name but didn't want to give him the pleasure of being remembered.

"Jim Richards, Senator. I'm with the New York Times."

"Oh, yes. The New York Times. My wife was terribly sick this morning, so I had to stay with her. I thought I'd have to take her to the hospital, but she began to feel better by mid-morning."

Charles thought of that lie earlier. It wasn't a lie because his pathetic wife felt bad every morning. It probably had something to do with how much she drank the night before. Every night before.

"I'm glad to know you're such a caring family man," the reporter said as he leaned back in the chair. "So, what do you think of this pipeline issue?"

"I'll be giving a statement to the press tomorrow, Mr. Robbins. You'll hear my opinion then."

The reporter pushed the chair back and stood. "That's Mr. Richards, Senator. Jim Richards. Wouldn't you like to share a little something with the millions of readers who will be looking at our paper first thing in the morning?" He opened a small notebook and pulled a pen out of his pocket.

"Tell them we are doing everything we can to advance American prosperity while maintaining the ecological health of our wonderful natural resources. I hope you'll be at the press conference tomorrow."

Richards slammed his notebook closed and thrust the pen back into his pocket. "Good day, Senator."

Charles watched him leave before quickly eating his sandwich. He realized he'd not have privacy here, so he hurried down the street to Stanton Park before pulling out his phone again.

"You have an update, Reggie?" Charles said into his phone.

"She's coming around, Boss. Don't you worry. I wouldn't count on tonight, but she'll be good as new by tomorrow. We had Dr…"

"I don't want to know who you had come over, Reggie," Charles interrupted. "Understand? I just want to know everything is okay. Got it?"

"Yes, sir, Mr. Fields."

"I also don't ever want to hear my name on your lips again. Is that clear?"

"Yes sir, Boss. All good here. You want us to bring in another girl tonight?"

Charles thought about it for a moment. "No, well, if one falls in your lap, I suppose that would be okay. Focus on getting the one you have out of the woods. You're about to get us into some hot water. I don't want any trouble. Understand?"

"We don't have any trouble. The girl's just a little smaller than we figured. That's all. I stuck her with a little more…"

"You shouldn't have stuck her a second time, you idiot. I don't want to hear about it, Reggie. I told you that. Just get her on her feet. I have a meeting early in the morning, so I want her functioning well by tomorrow night."

"You know we usually keep them…"

"I know how compliant they usually are, and that's fine. I'll plan to meet her tomorrow night after 10:00."

Charles disconnected the call and started to throw his phone at a tree until he noticed a little girl staring from the playground. He slipped the phone into his pocket and turned to walk back to the Russell building. This day had been a disaster.

Chapter Four

Jon and Meg stood as Jennifer rushed into the room. Michael followed with a phone stuck to his ear. Meg heard enough of Michael's conversation to know he must be talking to someone at his office.

"Oh, Jon, I'm so sorry we weren't here when you arrived. It's so good to see you." Jennifer hugged him.

"No problem, Jennifer," Jon said.

"Well, we should have been here. I mean it looks like we're not happy to see you, but we are. Michael and I have been anticipating celebrating Christmas with you for a while, haven't we, Michael?"

Jennifer turned to see her husband on the phone. She dismissed him with her hand and turned toward Meg. "So good to see you, Meg. You look so beautiful as always." The two women hugged.

"There's nothing like celebrating Christmas with family," Meg said. *I suppose technically we're not real family.* "I thought Gina told me Kate was here, too. She must be coming later."

"Oh, well, she's, well, she's here," Jennifer
stammered. "She just went out for a while. She'll
probably be back by dinner. She wanted to see a
friend in DC while we're here."

Meg caught Jon's eye before taking Jennifer's
hands. "We are so glad to see you. Lacy's bringing
her boyfriend up on Friday, and Carla's coming up
with Judy, too."

"I've heard so much about Lacy and Kerrick,"
Jennifer said. "It's all Kate can talk about.
Evidently, Kerrick is quite the specimen." Her face
began to change colors. "At least, that's how Kate
put it."

"I didn't realize Kate and Kerrick had met,"
Meg said.

"They haven't met. Maybe Lacy sent her a
picture."

"Or she's been Facebook stalking the poor
boy," Michael said as he clipped the phone to his
belt. He held his hand out to Jon. "Hey, Jon. Good
to see you." He turned and hugged Meg.

"Merry Christmas, Michael," Jon said. "So glad
we could join you guys. Gina had to go to some
event today but promised she'd be home in time
for dinner."

"Being First Lady has its share of
responsibilities," Michael said while pulling his
phone back out and looking at the screen. "Sorry.

I've got a big case coming up, and I need to respond to this text."

Jennifer watched Michael walk down the hall before she turned back to Jon and Meg. The three moved toward the couches and chairs. An attendant stepped in and offered them coffee.

"How have you been?" Jennifer asked. "I mean, you're world travelers and all. Last time I heard from you seems like you were going to Europe or Norway, or was it Mexico?"

Meg thought for a moment. "I think we were about to fly to Denmark, though we were in Mexico a few months ago."

"See what I mean. World travelers. I'm sorry. I didn't mean to make fun of you. Truth is I'm probably a little jealous because the only world I get to see is the west end of Richmond. I don't mean that the way it sounded. It sounds like I'm so ungrateful. I'm really not at all."

Sitting her coffee cup back in the saucer, Meg said, "You're fine, Jennifer. We have traveled a lot lately, but we're planning to settle down for a bit, aren't we, Jon?"

"Oh, yes. When we leave DC, we're heading back to our place in the Bahamas, and you won't be able to pry us out of there with a crowbar."

"How's Kate doing?" Meg asked.

Jennifer pulled her coffee cup to her lips, and Meg noticed it seemed to be shaking a bit. After a

long moment, Jennifer returned the cup to the
saucer and rung her hands as she cleared her throat.
"She's been okay. It's been a difficult semester for
her."

"I'm sure the University is quite challenging,"
Jon said.

Jennifer stared down at her lap. "To be honest,
we're having more problems with her. I don't even
want to bring our issues with her up because I don't
want to ruin everyone's Christmas. She's the reason
we weren't here when you arrived."

Meg saw a tear drop from Jennifer's cheek.
Something inside Meg broke, and she felt her own
eyes wet with unshed tears. What must it be like to
have a daughter you love so much rebel with such
determination? She thought of Carla and wondered
how she'd respond if her own sweet daughter acted
with such reckless selfishness.

Jennifer looked toward where they'd seen
Michael disappear before turning back to Jon and
Meg. "She did this last time we came up here and
ended up pregnant. Now, here we go again."

"I'm not following you," Meg said as she
moved over to sit beside Jennifer on the couch.
"Why don't you start at the beginning."

"Whatever you've heard about Kate you can
multiply by ten," Jennifer said. "She's out of
control. I suspect drugs, but I don't know that for
sure. Well, I know she's been smoking pot, but I

think she's into harder stuff. Her real problem is boys. Maybe some sex addiction or something."

Struggling with her own emotions, Meg placed her hand on Jennifer's arm. "I'm so sorry, Jennifer. I know your heart is broken."

"I'm so…" Jennifer stopped and looked at Meg as if frozen. Jennifer seemed hollow. Hopeless. Tears now flowed freely down her cheeks.

Meg pulled Jennifer into her arms and hugged her. "Oh, Jennifer. We'll help Kate any way we can."

"I'm not rescuing her this time, but I don't know what to do," Jennifer almost whispered. "I mean, Dad's running for reelection. Do you realize what would happen if it got out the President's granddaughter is out partying in DC and sleeping with any guy who will take her home?"

Jon moved to the chair beside Jennifer. "Where is she?"

"That's one of the problems. I don't know for sure. Her car was at a bar across town, but no one seems to know where she is."

Jon looked at his watch. "So, she's been gone for how long? Fifteen or sixteen hours?"

"She left here last night at 10:30. The Secret Service has a record of when she left last night." Jennifer looked at Jon and Meg and pulled her hands up as if she were about to pray. "Please don't make a big deal out of this. Michael and I are embarrassed, and I'm afraid Kate is embarrassing herself and doesn't even realize it."

Rising to his feet, Jon said, "She could be in trouble."

"No, Jon. Please. Sit down. She's not in trouble. Well, she's in trouble, but it's not like you think. We came to visit last February, and Kate did the same thing. She set it up to look like she was going out with friends, but she disappeared with some guy. She ended up getting pregnant over that experience and had an abortion. I know how you feel about abortion, but that's what happened. She had the abortion before I even knew she was pregnant."

Tears rolled down Meg's cheeks. "Jennifer…"

"I know," Jennifer interrupted. "It'll be just like last time. Give her a night or two, and she'll call us to come get her. I doubt we'll be able to bring her back here. Last time she was stoned out of her mind. If the media gets hold of this…"

"Jennifer, Kate is more important," Meg insisted. "We've got to find her before she does more to hurt herself."

"Please, Meg. I told you because I needed to tell someone, but please don't. Mom doesn't even know, and I'm not going to tell her. Kate will call soon, and we'll pick her up and take her back to Richmond. I'm sorry we've ruined Christmas. Maybe one of these days she'll grow up."

Chapter Five

Meg pushed the door closed behind them as she and Jon walked into the Lincoln bedroom. They'd stayed in this historic room the last time they visited Randall and Gina, but Meg still felt like she should take off her shoes or at least whisper. Even though the bed looked long enough for Lincoln to have slept in it, one of the hostesses had assured them on their last visit the room had only been an office for President Lincoln back in the 1860's.

However, Meg could barely think about the fact they were in the Lincoln bedroom in the White House. "Jon, we've got to do something."

"I agree. If nothing else, we need to go jerk Kate out of some guy's apartment or probably more like some room on skid row."

Meg walked over and sat down on the small couch against the wall. "If Jennifer and Michael would involve the authorities, they could probably watch video from the bar to see who she left with. We'd at least have somewhere to start."

"True," Jon agreed, "but you heard Jennifer. There's no way she's doing that."

"What if we do it?" Meg stood and began pacing around the room. "What if we could somehow convince the bar owner to let us watch the videos."

"Not likely he'd do that."

"What if you told him you were with the FBI or something like that?"

"Meg Davenport! I can't believe you're suggesting I tell a lie." Jon smiled and grabbed her hand. "You've got to quit pacing. You're stressing me out."

He pulled her into his arms and kissed her.

"Wow. What was that for?"

"The whole time we were talking to Jennifer was just a reminder to me of what a wonderful, precious treasure I have in you."

Meg looked into Jon's beautiful eyes and slid her hands into his hair. "That's the sweetest thing you've said today." She smiled and stood on her toes to kiss him again. "I wasn't being totally serious about the FBI thing, though there's got to be something we can do."

"What if I go down and talk with the Secret Service guy who saw Kate last night before she left? Maybe he would be willing to help us out, unofficially of course."

"Brilliant."

Jon grinned. "Today must be one of my better days." He pulled Meg into a hug and kissed her neck. "Umm. You smell great!"

"Jon Davenport. We've got a crisis on our hands, and you're focused on my perfume?"

"Okay, you're right. I suppose I'd better go talk with our Secret Service guy."

Fifteen minutes later, Meg's cell phone rang, and she saw it was Jon. "Hey. Why are you calling me? Everything okay?"

"Yeah. Ryan's going to help us out, but we have to go with him right now."

"Ryan? Is that the agent?"

"Yep. He can take a break, and he thinks he can get the guy to let us review the tapes. Of course, it'll have to be unofficial, but he thinks he can get the owner to cooperate. He knows who the owner is, but he doesn't really know him."

"Awesome. I'll grab my coat and be right down. Hopefully we can be back in time for dinner."

Ryan drove them across town in his personal SUV and pulled into the parking lot of McClanahan's. It was still early, so the bar wasn't busy. Meg figured their timing was perfect.

They entered the bar and asked to see the owner. Ryan flashed his badge but didn't hold it up long enough for the guy at the door to be able to read it. The man escorted them into an office.

"Mr. Reynolds. These folks need to speak with you. They're FBI."

Meg wanted to laugh. They never said they were FBI.

Ryan waited on the bouncer to leave. He held out his hand and the owner eventually reached out to shake. "Mr. Reynolds, I'm Ryan Butler."

"Cyrus Reynolds."

"And this is Jon and Meg," Ryan continued. He flashed his Secret Service identification. "We're not FBI, but we came by to help keep your fine establishment out of the papers and off the news."

"I'm not following."

"We need to talk unofficially so I won't have to turn in a report to my superiors. If we can do that, I think I can keep this little problem under wraps."

"What problem is that?"

"It has to do with underage patrons," Ryan lied. "We're willing to keep you out of it if you cooperate."

"We don't allow underage customers, Mr. Butler. I can assure you."

"We've been looking into your business," Ryan said, "and we're impressed with what we've found. That's why we're willing to cut you some slack. If we could view your video footage from last night, we'll verify what we need to know and be on our way. I can keep you out of it."

"You know you're supposed to have a warrant," Reynolds said.

"If you want us to get a warrant, Mr. Reynolds, we're happy to do that," Jon said. "We thought you'd rather keep this personal and just allow us to review the footage. That's all we want."

Meg was impressed. Jon was so smooth, though technically he was lying. She watched the owner's face shift and change before he finally nodded.

"Okay. Follow me."

The owner left them alone, and they spent the next hour fast-forwarding through digital video feed, starting at 10:30 the previous night. Kate appeared in the video at 10:42. They could tell as the evening progressed, she was getting tipsy and much too friendly with a guy.

"How many beers did she drink?" Meg asked.

"Too many," Ryan said.

Meg leaned toward the monitor. "She's getting up. I bet she's going to the restroom."

Sure enough. Kate staggered toward the restroom, falling on several customers in the process. One guy did something obscene, but Kate didn't seem to notice.

They watched for her to return, but she never did.

"Rewind the video, Ryan," Jon said. "Back to the place before Kate gets up."

They watched the two making out in a booth before Kate wiggled out and nearly fell on the floor. As Kate walked away, Meg noticed the guy looking at his phone.

"Looks like he's texting someone," Ryan said.

"I thought the same thing," Jon agreed.

Ryan continued playing the video, and they watched the guy slip out of the booth and walk out of the bar. He didn't seem to stagger at all.

"I bet we could go back and count the beers he drank and discover he only had a couple."

"She couldn't have spent the night in the bathroom," Meg said. "Keep the video going so we can see what happens."

They watched the video in fast motion as the customers eventually filed out. An employee walked into the women's restroom, came out, and turned off the light.

Meg felt the color drain from her face as the facts began to sink in. Kate hadn't gone home with anyone.

She'd been kidnapped.

Chapter Six

Jon shook Ryan's hand and thanked him, but he felt as clueless as he had before going to the bar. Meg slipped her hand into his and tugged gently.

"What are you going to do?" Ryan asked.

Jon's eyes locked with Meg's and offered a silent plea for patience before turning back to Ryan "I'm not sure. Let's think about the video for a second. We saw other people leaving. Is it possible she put on a disguise?"

Meg stepped toward him. "Why would she do that? I mean, who would she be hiding from?"

Ryan rubbed his chin and looked down. "It seems like I remember someone coming out of the bathroom and going further down the little hallway. You know, the opposite direction. I didn't think she resembled Kate, but she may have been a similar size."

"I vaguely remember that," Meg said, "but I'd need to see the video again."

"Seeing the video again might be a problem," Ryan said. "We could, but I have to be careful. The Secret Service has serious consequences for people using their credentials inappropriately."

"Jennifer, Kate's mother, told us this kind of activity is normal for Kate." Meg said. "She seems to have issues and disappearing with men is one of them."

Checking his watch, Ryan said, "I get off in the morning at seven o'clock. I'll go by McClanahan's and see if our buddy Cyrus will let me look at the video again."

"Will they be open at seven?" Jon asked.

Ryan shook his head. "Doubt it. That doesn't mean someone won't be around. I'll let you know."

Ryan walked away from them toward the West Wing entrance. Walking hand-in-hand across the frozen grass of the South Lawn, Meg and Jon talked about what they'd seen on the video.

"We can't wait until tomorrow morning," Meg insisted. "What if Kate's in trouble?"

"If we spill the beans to Gina and get law enforcement involved, and Kate ends up being shacked up in some apartment doped out of her mind, Jennifer and Michael will be livid."

"But what if she ends up being in serious trouble, and we're sitting here in the White House of the United States doing nothing with all these resources?"

Jon stopped and looked at Meg. "I think we need to talk with Jennifer and Michael, tell them what we've found out and try to get them to let Gina in on it."

"We could go back to the bar tonight," Meg said, "and look for the guy we saw in the video. I could even go in by myself to see if he hits on me. What if he steals girls or gets them involved in drugs?"

Jon shook his head and squeezed her hand. "No way. You're not going in there as bait. Let's talk to Jennifer and Michael."

The elevator door opened on the second floor of the White House residence where Gina stood waiting to greet them.

"Just in time for dinner," Gina said as Jon and Meg stepped out of the elevator and gave her hugs. "Actually, you have about fifteen minutes to freshen up if you'd like."

"Is the meal formal?" Meg asked.

Gina laughed. "Honey, I try to be informal every opportunity I can, and this week is informal. Well, mostly."

"Great. We like informal," Meg said. "Where are Jennifer and Michael?"

Gina's smile left her face. "They had to leave. It seems Michael had some work emergency, and they had to go back to Richmond. They said they'd be back by Friday."

Jon saw Meg look at him before returning her gaze to the floor. "We'll clean up and see you at dinner."

Jon opened the door of the bedroom and laid the suitcases on the bed. Meg walked to their luggage, pulled out clothes, and put them into a dresser.

"Do you really think Jennifer and Michael had to go home for his work?" Meg asked.

"I doubt it. I bet they're driving around looking for Kate. They may end up going home once they find her."

"That's what I figured, too," Meg said as she stepped to the sink in the bathroom.

"Do I smell like smoke?" Jon asked.

"What?" I can't hear you for the water.

Jon stepped behind Meg and wrapped his arms around her. She felt warm. Inviting. "Do I smell like smoke? You know, from the bar?"

Meg turned around, sniffed his shirt, and pulled it over his head. "Yep. You're a regular smokestack." She rubbed her hands on his chest. "You could just go shirtless. Gina said we're being informal."

Jon kissed her and laughed. "That would be quite a shock. I'll put on a clean shirt."

Meg walked back into the bedroom and called Jennifer. After trying twice, she left a message asking Jennifer to call her.

"Now what, Jon? We can't sit here tonight and act like nothing's wrong."

"We need to tell Gina."

"I agree, but I think we should go to the bar first."

"Meg, you're not going in there to try to catch some sex trafficker."

"Jon, that's not what I want to do. I want to go in and see if this same guy tries to pick me up. If he does, we'll know something's up. I can talk to him for a minute and slip into the restroom. When I go to the restroom, you talk to the guy.

Jon looked at his watch. "Our fifteen minutes are up. We'll talk about it after dinner, but I don't like your idea."

"It's not dangerous, Jon. What could happen? You'll be in there with me. We're out there in plain view of everyone else in the bar."

Although they enjoyed conversation around the dinner table for a while, Jon felt troubled over his earlier conversation with Meg. Should they do anything about Kate or just ride it out? Gina had to retire early to work on a speech she had to give, so she hugged them both and headed down the hall to her office.

As Jon and Meg left the dining area, Meg picked up the conversation about Kate as if it had never been interrupted with dinner. Arguing in whispers, they walked to their bedroom.

"No way, Meg. It's too dangerous."

"Come on, Jon. Like you said, she's probably stoned out of her mind in some guy's bed. It won't hurt to ask a few questions."

"What if we find the guy, and he's involved in a kidnapping ring? What then? Am I supposed to ask him to give her back?"

Meg wrapped her arms around Jon's waist. "Jon, you know how to ask questions without making it look like you're accusing him of anything. Being smooth is your forte."

Jon frowned. "I'm not for it."

"Kate could be in trouble, Jon. I'll wear a wire."

"A what?"

"Isn't that what they call it? I'll walk in by myself but wear a device so you can keep up with me the whole time. We've got to at least try."

Jon stared at her in silence, and Meg dropped her hands to her side and walked back into the bathroom. He heard water come on and the sounds of Meg brushing her teeth. Sitting down onto the couch, he leaned his head back.

What could they do? Meg was right about one thing. Kate could be in trouble, and no one was doing anything about it. He heard the water come on in the shower. It was early, and Meg was taking a shower. Not a good sign.

He'd angered her, but she seemed clueless about the dangers. If something bad happened to Kate, it could happen to Meg.

He considered the possibilities of Meg's idea. If they got a tracking device so there was no way she disappeared, he'd feel better about agreeing with her.

Meg came out of the bathroom wearing a robe with her hair wrapped up in a towel.

Jon stood. "Meg, I'll call Jose. He was in the special forces in Spain. He'll know what to do."

Jon loved Jose like a brother. They'd become close friends a few years earlier when he saved Meg from thugs trying to get information on the whereabouts of sunken treasure in the Bahamas. Jose ended up marrying Meg's best friend and becoming Jon's partner in the salvage business.

Meg walked toward him and wrapped her arms around him. "I love you, Jon, and I know you're trying to do the right thing."

Their lips met, and Jon felt Meg melting into him. She pulled back and rested her head on his chest.

"Were you more upset about Kate or that I disagreed with you?" Jon asked.

"Maybe both. I will feel better knowing Kate's okay, however."

Meg pulled away and reached for her phone. She held it out, and Jon saw Jose's number on the screen. He smiled, pulled out his own phone, and called his best friend and partner.

As he talked to Jose, Jon walked down the hallway. He sat down in the living room and shared the details of the situation. When he returned, he noticed Meg had gotten dressed as if she were going out.

"He's calling a contact he has here in DC," Jon said. "As long as you don't get out of my sight, and as long as you wear a tracker, I'll go along with it."

Meg sat down beside him and kissed his cheek. "Thank you, Jon. Nothing bad will happen. You'll see."

Chapter Seven

From a block away, Jon and Meg stared at the front door of McClanahan's. They watched their new friend, a stocky, Hispanic man, walk into the bar. She felt Jon's hand in hers, reassuring her she wouldn't be alone. How Jose managed to put together a two-man surveillance so quickly was a mystery to them.

Meg had always teased Jose about knowing people all over the world, and his knowledge seemed true tonight. Jon had placed the phone call to Jose, and in no time, he called back with everything lined up. She reached into the pocket of her jacket and felt the small transmitter that was connected to a tiny device she'd sewn into the hem of her shirt.

Jon looked at her and winked. "You know I don't like you going into that place wearing that shirt. Every man there is going to stare."

"That's kind of the point, isn't it? It's not inappropriate. I'm supposed to look like a swinging college student who just moved to town."

"You certainly look the part," Jon said. He reached out to move a strand of hair behind her

ear. "Everyone already believes I robbed the
cradle."

"I suppose I'll appreciate that comment in
another twenty years."

Jon leaned over and kissed her. "I still don't like
it."

"We just watched Alberto walk in. You know I
won't be alone." She pointed to a U-Haul rental
van down the road. "Plus, my every move is being
followed."

They'd talked briefly with Jose's friends, and
Meg knew they were well-trained, former special
ops guys. Alberto agreed to go into the bar ten
minutes ahead of her and blend in with the crowd
with Brian tracking her every step through a
monitor in the U-Haul.

"I'm still coming in after you've had time to
settle," Jon insisted. "No one will know I'm your
husband." He looked down at her hand. "Give me
your rings. That diamond and gold band would
definitely blow your cover."

Meg smiled and looked up at Jon. "I don't
know which feels weirder, taking my rings off or
walking into a bar to get picked up by another
man."

"Like I said, I don't like it. I think we should
call the whole thing off."

"Jon, we can't. Kate's life may be in danger. All we're doing is scoping out the place, and then we'll call Jennifer."

"And if we can't get her, we're spilling it all to Gina. We should have already involved her, the FBI, and police."

"If we do this right, we may be able to locate her and get her back tonight without alerting the media. We won't anger Jennifer, and Randall's name won't be mentioned on the news, at least not about this unfortunate issue."

"If Kate's shacked up with someone shooting up with who knows what," Jon said through clenched teeth, "I'll throttle her myself."

"Yeah, let's hope that's it. Well, I guess we shouldn't hope for drugs and sex for anyone, especially Kate. We've had enough issues in the past with Lacy." Meg looked down at her watch. "Show time." She reached for the door handle. "I love you, Jon. I'll be fine."

"I'm coming in after a while," Jon said.

"Give me an hour, please. I might accidentally look at you and give us away. Alberto's in there, and I'm wearing a wire. I'm going to hang onto my jacket all night. I'll be fine."

"Hang onto your jacket?"

"Yes. I couldn't figure out the best place to hide the transmitter. Right now, it's in the pocket of my jacket. I should have clipped it under my shirt, but I felt like someone might notice it, and these jeans are too tight."

"See what I mean about the shirt?" Jon said. "And I didn't mention the jeans. Did you take the tags off?"

"Before we left the store tonight."

Meg walked through the door of McClanahan's and felt a little self-conscious and nervous. She noticed several guys staring at her and saw one lean over and say something to his buddy. Maybe this wasn't a good idea. Then again, Kate may need her.

One problem she would face quickly was having to decide what to order. She hated the taste of alcohol but knew she couldn't avoid ordering a drink. Jon had instructed her on what to order and had given her a glass bottle filled with Mountain Dew to carry in her purse. Maybe it would work.

She ordered a drink and a clean glass and carried them to an empty table where she'd spotted several empty bottles. It didn't take long for a young man to claim the chair across from her. He had to be ten years younger than her. She didn't know whether to be flattered or offended.

They made small talk for a while before she told him she was expecting someone. Thankfully, he left her table.

Meg looked across the room and saw the guy from the video. He was talking to the bartender.

She tried averting her gaze, but out of the corner of her eye noticed him strolling her way.

"You expecting someone?" Video Guy stood at her table.

Meg felt her mouth go dry. Everything hinged on how well she was able to sell herself. She eyed the half-empty bottle of Mountain Dew in front of her and hoped no one noticed the glass of alcohol in the chair beside her. She'd pushed it far enough under the table so no one would see it.

Meg wrapped her hands around the glass in front of her and brought the Mountain Dew to her lips. "Uh, no, not really."

"Not really?"

"I just moved to town," Meg said hesitantly. "I don't know people, and I heard this was a good place to make friends."

"I'm Brad," the guy said as he pulled out a chair.

"Melissa." Meg hadn't thought about what name to use, but Melissa would work as good as anything else.

Could Kate be at this guy's apartment spaced out on drugs? Possibly. Then again, if she were there, why would Brad be here?

"So, you just moved to town?"

"Yeah. From LA, as in Lower Alabama." Meg grinned. "I came here hoping to get a job and find a fresh start. I just don't know anyone yet, but I'm determined not to return to Alabama. Ever."

"That bad?"

"Worse. I didn't tell my parents where I was going. As if they cared." Meg rehearsed that line earlier knowing it would set her up as a prospect for being kidnapped, if that was indeed what had happened to Kate. It may also set her up as a good, one-night stand. "But hey," Meg faked a belch. "Excuse me. I'm in DC, and everything's about to change for good. Right?"

"Sounds good to me. DC is a great place for starting over. Opportunities abound." He looked at the empty bottles. "Looks like you're celebrating."

"Yeah. Trying to." Meg giggled, trying to convince Brad she'd had too much to drink. She pointed to the bottle. "This one is number four, or maybe five, so I need to stop. I start getting a little buzz after two."

For the next twenty minutes, Brad talked about his job as a lobbyist, which Meg didn't believe for a minute. She sipped on her Mountain Dew and slurred a word occasionally. She looked across the room and noticed Alberto watching. All was well. Thank heavens Jon hadn't walked in yet.

Meg noticed Alberto look at his watch and touch his ear. He slipped from the bar stool and hurried toward the door. He must have forgotten to tell Brian something.

She tried to learn from Brad how often he came to the bar and whether he knew some of the people who frequented the place. He didn't seem to want to divulge anything.

"You want to dance?" Brad asked.

Meg didn't want to dance with anyone but her husband. "Sure." Meg stood, wobbling for effect. "I've got to go to the lady's room first." Going to the restroom would buy some time, but she'd have to come up with a plan for not getting too close to this guy.

As she pushed opened the bathroom door, she realized she'd left her jacket on the back of her chair. Hopefully, the transmitter could connect from this distance. She'd be back to her table in a minute and wouldn't part with her jacket again.

Chapter Eight

Jon looked at his watch for the thirtieth time in twenty minutes. The longer he sat in his car the less he liked this idea. He looked around and noticed homeless people and drunks sitting around in the shadows of storefronts. His beautiful wife was in the bar giving herself as human bait, and he sat useless in the car.

Odds are Kate disappeared with some guy and will show up tomorrow or the next day. There's no need to get worked up. Meg's fine, and Alberto is in there watching her every move.

He wouldn't swear on it, but he felt confident he watched a drug deal go down about twenty feet from his car. He should have gone in with Meg. What was he thinking?

Jon looked at his watch again. He'd told her he was giving her thirty minutes before coming in even though she'd asked for an hour. It had been twenty-five. That was enough. He had to get Meg, and they were going back to the White House and getting Gina out of bed. Time to come clean.

Grabbing the car key, Jon reached for the door handle and stepped into the night. He looked down the road toward the bar. He heard a noise behind him, but before he could turn around, an explosion of pain burst in his head. Jon collapsed and everything went black.

* * * * *

Alberto rushed out the door and ran toward Jon's car. He saw Brian land a kick to a guy's chest and catch a second mugger with an elbow to his face. Jon's body lay on the ground.

By the time Alberto made it to the car, the two thugs were out cold, and his friend was bent over Jon's still form. Blood flowed from a gash on the back of Jon's head.

"Call an ambulance," Brian said. "They hit him hard."

Alberto grabbed his phone and punched 911. Dispatch told him an officer was one block away. As Alberto started back for the bar, the officer rounded the corner. He figured the cop would want his perspective on things, so he stayed.

Brian told Alberto the 911 dispatcher was sending an ambulance. The two men explained to the officer how Jon had been mugged, and they just happened to be walking by. Both men knew Jon and Meg were trying to keep the police out of this issue with President Johnson's granddaughter, so they kept some facts to themselves.

"Officer, are you done with me?" Alberto asked. "I've got to go to the bathroom."

"Sure," the policeman said. "This is the third mugging I've dealt with tonight. Hopefully this man will be okay." The officer put cuffs on the two men who lay moaning on the ground.

An ambulance pulled up, and two paramedics began working with Jon who had begun to stir. Another paramedic checked on the two muggers. Alberto needed to get back inside and retrieve Meg. They'd have to come back and finish this charade another time.

"Brian, I'm heading into McClanahan's," Alberto said. "I'll see you inside."

Alberto walked through the door back into the dimly lit bar. He spotted the guy Meg had been with walking across the room. He squinted through the gloom. *Where's Meg.* He saw the guy grab a woman's hand. *There she is. Be careful, Meg.*

Alberto settled back down at the small table and continued watching. Meg pulled the guy toward the crowded dance floor. She played the part well.

A voice came through his earbud. "Hey, Alberto. They're taking Jon to the hospital for some stitches and to check him out. Get Meg and meet us there."

Alberto spoke into the small microphone hidden in the collar of his jacket. "She's with the subject right now. I'll blow her cover if I interrupt. I'll get her out as soon as possible."

"You know Jon's not going to be happy if you let this go on much longer."

"She's okay. You know how hospitals are anyway. It'll be a while before they do anything. Are they taking him to George Washington?"

"Yep. Don't wait too long. Jon's going to be ticked."

Alberto sat back and watched Meg through the gloom. Moving closer would improve his perspective, but maybe hiding behind the darkness was better.

The couple danced through several songs, and Alberto began to squirm. He had to get her to the hospital. It also bothered him that Meg sure seemed to be snuggling up with this guy. Play acting was one thing, but her actions were over the top.

They were on the other side of the room dancing, so maybe she wasn't coming onto him like it appeared. His eyes scanned the room and landed on her jacket draped over the back of the chair.

After a bit more, Alberto decided he had to step in and get Meg to the hospital. He knew of no way to do it accept to barge in on a dance. He thought of asking for a dance but doing so might start something that could get ugly.

He walked across the room where Meg was dancing with the guy. "Meg. There you are." He reached out and touched her on the shoulder.

The woman turned around and stared blankly at him. She wasn't Meg.

Chapter Nine

Reggie sped across town and checked his rearview mirror occasionally to make sure the woman remained unconscious. After the screw up the night before, he had eased up on the dosage of the shot. The drug should keep her out for a while.

He thought of the close call with the girl from the previous night. The last thing he needed was a dead body. She was going to be okay. He grinned. *As okay as one of those girls can be.* The truth was she was more than okay. She was hot. He wondered if he could bid on her in the auction.

Reggie knew the senator had a temper, but he'd never experienced his anger like he had earlier that day. Bringing in this prize he had in the back would certainly make his boss happy. She was a beauty queen, sure to bring top dollar. Two beautiful women in two nights was a real score.

Traffic was light, and it didn't take him too long to get out to Shady Oak. He drove in front of the senator's stately, old mansion and turned into a private drive that took him down the side of the property.

He pulled through the gate to the carriage house and slipped through the open garage door, which closed behind him. The dome light came on inside the van as he slid open the door and illuminated the woman's beautiful face. Reggie had already sent a picture of her to the boss, but he took a second one for good measure. He always sent his boss a picture of the girl so the senator could anticipate his sampling of the merchandise.

The senator's rules weren't fair. He told Reggie at least once a week, "No one is to touch the girls!" But Reggie knew the senator didn't follow his own rules. Oh, well. At least the pay was good. He got $500 per girl, which was quite sweet. He usually brought in five or six per week. One day, he was going to live in a fine house in the Caribbean.

He eyed the tape around the woman's wrists and checked her pulse. Slow but steady, sleeping like a baby, and she was a babe, for sure. She was a little older than the girl the night before, but the senator always liked variety. He tried to guess her age. Maybe twenty-three or twenty-four.

Expecting to see the boss heading his way, he looked toward the house. Reggie figured Senator Fields would rather have this one than the girl he'd brought in the previous night. Of course, his boss didn't want Reggie ever to say his name. Dumb. It's not like he didn't know Charles Fields was the boss and a U. S. Senator. Reggie didn't care. Where else could he bring home $3,000 a week?

He grinned. Maybe, if the senator wanted this one, Reggie could have the one from last night. She should be alert and ready by now. He looked at his watch and back to the house. What was taking the boss so long? Senator Fields had to know when the van arrived.

The senator's wife would be in bed now, so the old guy would be alone. Reggie decided he'd go up to the house and enter through the employee's entrance. Maybe his first picture was lost in cyberspace.

Reggie had things to do and needed to get on with it, unless his boss was going to let him enjoy the spoils. He checked the woman one more time and saw she was definitely out cold. He'd be right back. She'd be fine.

* * * * *

Charles looked at the picture again and turned on his computer. Something about her looked familiar, but he couldn't figure it out. *All these girls start looking familiar. You know that.*

He booted up his laptop and scanned through his files. If he had seen this woman, it would be because he had a picture of her. The only reason he'd have a picture was if she was connected to someone he'd planned to bring down.

Several prospects came to mind, but the number one person on his personal hate list was Randall Johnson. Charles had several projects in the works that would prevent him from winning re-election.

He smiled as he thought about one strategy that would get Johnson out of office for sure. He'd learned in Washington truth didn't matter. All he had to do was stir up enough people, connect the President to an implied indiscretion, and President Johnson's political future would be over.

Charles opened the file and scanned several pictures he'd saved over the last few years. Pinning something to Johnson had been tricky. He'd never known a politician to be so clean. The President must have paid good money for someone to scrub his past from the internet.

He spotted a folder entitled *Family* and nearly fell out of his chair. He cursed and slammed his fist onto the desk. He looked back at the picture on his phone. Reggie was a fool. He should kill him for being so stupid. Meg Davenport may as well be President Johnson's daughter.

He glared at the picture from his file again of the president walking Meg down the aisle at her wedding in the Bahamas. He tried to remember something important about her, maybe about her

husband. It came to him. They were treasure
hunters and had struck it rich.

Charles stopped on an article from the Atlanta
Journal that focused on Jon Davenport. *Real Estate
tycoon? Impressive. He was quite wealthy before finding
Spanish treasure. From college professor to what?
Billionaire? Probably.*

It struck Charles that all Davenport had to do
was alert Randall Johnson. His skin crawled at the
thought of the president. If Johnson got involved,
Charles knew his whole operation was at risk.

The security light beside his computer began to
blink. Someone was at the backdoor. Probably
Reggie. Charles opened his desk drawer and pulled
out his Walther PDP pistol. This latest foul up
would be Reggie's last.

The senator stood. Paused. Killing Reggie here
might make things dicey. For one thing, he had two
girls in the basement and more at the warehouse. If
Reggie were out of the picture, he'd be short a
helper for the project. He'd have to get too
involved with keeping his merchandise drugged
before the sale tomorrow night. That wouldn't
work.

Slipping the small pistol into his pocket, Charles
headed toward the back door where he peered
through the window at Reggie's stupid face. Heat
crept up the back of his neck, and he thought he
might strip a gear. Why did he always seem to hire

idiots? It's like he was surrounded by them in the Senate and in his personal enterprise.

"What did you think?" Reggie asked as the door opened. He had a stupid grin on his face. "You told me to get one if she fell in my lap. Well, this beauty was dropped in front of me from heaven."

"Hello, Reggie," Charles said with measured patience. "Come into my study."

Charles noticed Reggie's puffed-up chest. He stood a little taller. *He better enjoy his last two days on earth!*

Chapter Ten

Meg felt a sharp pain as her head hit something hard. She tried to open her eyes, but they didn't want to cooperate. What was going on? It appeared she was in a vehicle, probably a van, and the van was moving. She tried to move her hands but couldn't. She moved her finger toward her wrist and touched tape with the tip of her finger. Probably duct tape. She couldn't move her legs. Her ankles must be taped, too. She lay still and tried to remember the events of the evening.

She'd been at the bar to figure out what happened to Kate. She'd gone to the bathroom. *What happened in the restroom? I can't remember.*

She thought about the tracker in the seam of her shirt but realized the transmitter was in her coat pocket. Meg remembered Brian saying the tracker was only good for a short distance without the transmitter. *I left my coat at my chair. Dumb.*

Whatever happened, she'd been drugged. Whoever was driving this van wanted her unconscious. She needed to stay awake, but everything in her kept trying to drag her back into a pit of darkness. She had to fight it. *If I go to sleep, this guy may kill me.*

Her mind went back to when terrorists had kidnapped her in Miami. Those guys had a lot of tools in the van, including a box cutter. What were the odds tools would be in this van? Maybe if she lay still, she'd have an opportunity to escape.

Sometime later, Meg jerked awake, realizing she'd dozed off. How had that happened? *Someone gave you something to make you sleep, Meg. How do you think it happened?*

She realized that other than having her hands and feet bound, she wasn't tied to anything. Whoever took her wasn't too bright.

Sitting up, Meg felt like the world was spinning out of control. She felt nauseous. She closed her eyes and sat still a few moments. *Okay. Move slowly. Maybe you can find something in the van to cut the tape.*

Meg opened her eyes and peered through the darkness. Nothing. She got on her knees, her right shoulder on the floor of the van, and managed to scoot around the empty space. No tools. Only a bench seat and probably two seats up front.

She needed something sharp. She felt the leg of the seat and moved her hand upward. About a foot or two off the floor, the seat frame turned, and a piece of metal stuck out. It had a tiny, sharp point.

Meg stretched the tape onto the point. It took several attempts, but she tugged her hands free and tore the tape from around her ankles.

She had to get away.

She slid open the side door of the van, and the dome light came on, lighting the single-car garage. Meg cringed at the thought of someone seeing her.

She left the door open a moment to inspect her surroundings. It looked like storage rooms on each side and a door in front of the van. She tried to open the garage door, but it wouldn't budge. Maybe she'd find a window somewhere.

After closing the van door and being wrapped in darkness again, Meg tried the doorknob to the storage room. The knob turned. She eased inside, careful not to stumble over anything. She held onto the door frame for a moment as she waited for everything to stop spinning.

Light from the moon came through the sides of a curtain on the other side of the room. *A window.*

Meg pulled the curtain back, unlocked the window, and slid it up. She was about to heave herself through the opening when she heard voices. Angry voices. Someone was coming her way.

Oh, God. Help me. She couldn't get away. She only needed another minute or two, but time was up.

* * * * *

Charles felt like he was going to explode. Reggie was a walking dead man, but Charles didn't know if he could wait two more days to kill him, auction or not.

"I can't believe you left her out here in the van," Charles seethed. "Do you have any brains in your thick head?"

"I'm sorry. I had no idea she was related to the president. You don't have to worry, Mr. Fields. She's out cold."

Charles jerked the pistol out of his pocket and placed it against Reggie's head. "If I ever hear my name coming from your mouth again, you're a dead man. Got it?"

Reggie stared up at the pistol and held his hands out. "I'm, I'm sorry, Mr., uh, Boss. I won't ever say your name again. I don't even know your name."

Charles stared at him and thought about the inconvenience of getting rid of Reggie's lifeless body tonight. He lowered the pistol and returned it to his pocket.

"She'd better be out here and still unconscious."

"She will be. She's taped up, and I shot her with...what's that stuff? Keta something. Whatever. I shot her just like all the other times."

Charles slipped his key into the door. *At least he had enough sense to lock the door.* He strode through a small kitchen to a door that led to the garage. Flipping the light switch, he stepped inside. Reggie

moved to the side door of the van and opened it.
Meg Davenport was gone.

Charles let out a string of curse words as he
turned on the shorter man. He swung his fist and
connected with Reggie's face. Reggie fell against the
side of the van and covered his head with his arms
to protect himself from another blow.

"Where is she, Reggie?" Charles asked through
gritted teeth.

"She was here. She must have woke up." Reggie
saw the open door to the storage room. "She must
be in there."

Charles hurried through the door and saw the
open window. He couldn't believe his luck. She
must have just crawled through the window before
they came out of the house.

"Reggie, you'd better find her immediately. Do
you hear me? I'm calling Gage to come help you.
He's in the basement."

"She's got to be around here, Boss. She couldn't
have gone far. Besides, it's not like you've got any
neighbors to worry about."

Charles started to hit the idiot again, but his fist
hurt, and he needed Reggie to find Meg. He pulled
out his cell phone and walked back toward the
house as he dialed Gage's number. Gage wasn't
much brighter than Reggie, but maybe the two
could find a half-drugged woman stumbling around
in the night.

He looked behind him and saw Reggie run out of the carriage house with a flashlight. Charles shook his head as his phone connected. "Gage. You need to get out here to the backyard."

He listened for a moment. "You can finish tonight's medication later. We've got an emergency."

Chapter Eleven

Jon bolted upright in the hospital bed, leaned over, and vomited into a bowl. His head pounded, and he saw blood on the pillow.

"Dr. Davenport," a young nurse said. "You can't sit up like that. You probably have a concussion. You can't fall asleep again, either. You've got to stay with me. Of course, you're a doctor; so you know that."

Jon reached for the back of his head. "Not MD. PhD—History."

"No, don't touch your wound," the nurse said. "The doctor will sew that up, but I've got to clean it first. You took a nasty blow." The nurse reached for a cup of water on the bedside table. "You may want to rinse your mouth out."

Jon swirled water around in his mouth and spit into the bowl. He looked at his wrist, but someone had taken his watch. "What happened?"

"You were mugged," the nurse said. "You'll be okay, but you need stitches. I've got to get you cleaned up, and the doctor will be in shortly. He's busy, though. The crazies are out tonight. I'm Emma, by the way."

"Jon Davenport. Thanks for helping me."

"So, you're a professor?"

"I used to be. Now, I'm in real estate, and my wife and I run a salvage business in the Bahamas. Where is my wife?"

Emma pulled his hair back to inspect the wound. "I don't know. Probably out in the waiting area. We're not letting visitors back right now because we're so busy. Could you lie on your stomach so I can clean out this wound? Oh, wait a minute. Let me get a clean pillow and bowl. I'll be right back."

The nurse hurried out of the room, and Jon leaned over. He placed his hands on each side of his head as if squeezing or holding it together. How had he been mugged? He remembered getting out of the car to go into McClanahan's, but that's it. Someone had obviously hit him from behind.

He and Meg never should have attempted to go to that bar to get information on Kate. That was a dumb idea. He thought that by having Alberto and Brian there, they'd be okay. Remembering the creepy neighborhood around the bar, he realized just being in that place was a mugging waiting to happen. He was glad to be away from there. Of course, Meg was sitting out in the waiting room, and a hospital waiting room may not be much safer. At least Alberto and Brian were with her.

Emma returned with a clean pillow and began cleaning up the back of Jon's head. He felt her rinsing the area and dabbing it with gauze. "I'm sorry your welcoming committee wasn't the sort of people who make us proud here in Washington. It can be a dangerous place, especially at night."

"We shouldn't have been out," Jon said. "We were…well, it's a long story."

"You must have family here in Washington. Are you spending Christmas here?"

Jon almost told her he was visiting President Johnson but caught himself. Revealing that bit of news probably wouldn't be a good idea. He changed the subject.

"I suppose bad guys live everywhere," Jon said. "We live on an island in the Bahamas and have crooks there, too."

"Oh, I'd love to go to the Bahamas," Emma gushed. "I've always dreamed of it. So, if you have a salvage business, that means you scuba dive?"

"That's right. I've been diving for years. Maybe you could come down and visit us sometime." Emma smiled, and he figured she thought he was just making small talk. "I'm serious. We've got a guest house. During the summer, we run a program for inner-city boys and typically have a few interns helping. We love having guests. Are you married?"

"No. I was dating someone, but we broke up."

"Well, that settles it," Jon said. "Come stay with us, and we'll take you scuba diving. In fact, if you want a summer job, I'll hire you as our ship's nurse."

Jon felt Emma's hands still. "Are you serious?"

"Dead serious. I'll match your pay from here and give you free room and board. Can you take the summer off?"

"Dr. Davenport, if it means spending the summer on a boat in the Bahamas, I'd quit this place in a heartbeat. Besides, they're so desperate for nurses here that they'd give me three months off if I promised to return."

"Sounds like a deal. I'll give you my phone number, and you call me after Christmas. I'll send you some paperwork to complete, and we'll start making plans for a fun summer. I promise it will be an adventure."

Emma pulled out her cell phone and typed in the number Jon gave her. She was so excited he thought she might burst.

"The doctor will be in shortly to look at your wound and stitch it up," Emma finally said. "I'll be back after a while."

Jon lay still and soon felt himself drifting off. He remembered Nurse Emma saying he shouldn't sleep, so he decided to pray. He prayed for Kate, Jennifer, and Michael. He thanked God for Meg, Carla, Judy, Jose and Ann, Lacy and Kerrick, and every blessing that came to mind. As he prayed, he heard a buzzing in the room, but he tried to ignore it.

"Dr. Davenport, I'm Dr. Garcia."

Jon rolled over and sat up. He noticed from the clock on the wall he'd been in the room for a little more than an hour. A middle-aged man with greying hair stood beside him, his hand outstretched.

Jon reached out to shake his hand. "Hello Dr. Garcia. I'm sorry I had to come here to meet you."

"Me, too. I'd like to take a look at your wound before I sew it up."

Dr. Garcia tugged a little around the wound before Jon felt several stings in his head. He figured the doctor was giving him shots of Lidocaine to numb the area before sewing him up.

"Okay," the doctor finally said. "Looks good. Do you mind sitting up so I can look at your eyes?" The doctor pulled out a small light and inspected Jon's pupils. "Umm. Okay. You took a rough knock on the head, but I think you'll be okay. Do you have family here? I'd like to talk with them about your care for tonight."

"My wife and a couple of friends are in the waiting room," Jon said.

As if Jon conjured him with his comment, Alberto hurried into the room. His face was ashen.

The doctor saw Alberto's concern and looked back toward Jon. "I've got to check on the patient in the next room. I'll come back and speak with your friend."

As the door closed, Alberto stepped toward the bed. "Jon! I've been looking everywhere for you. I've called you and Brian and couldn't get either of you. Brian told me you were going to George Washington. I had no idea you were at Georgetown."

"No problem," Jon said. "I assume Brian's out in the waiting room."

"He is, but listen," Alberto pleaded. "We've got a problem."

Chapter Twelve

Meg rolled out from under the van after watching the two men hurry out of the garage. She had to get away. They'd be back, and she'd better be long gone.

They had come through the door in front of the van, so she stepped through it into a small kitchen area. The door leading outside stood open. Meg could see a large house on the other side of a huge yard lined with massive trees. Looking across the room, she noticed another window that opened away from the house. She opened the window and pulled herself through it.

She eased the window closed and crouched in the shadow of the garage. Searching for the best way to escape, she scanned her surroundings. She thought of Kate. *I can't run away. Kate could be in danger. If she's here, right now may be my only chance of getting her out alive.*

She looked around the corner of the building and saw an older man walking toward the main house. The other guy was searching a nearby stand of trees. She eyed the woods in front of her suspecting she could get closer to the main house unseen if she ran through the trees.

Meg hustled across the opening and squatted safely behind a large tree. She took a deep breath and steadied herself against the tree trunk. *Come on. No time for a break.* She stood and dashed through the trees toward the side of the main house.

A basement door opened, and Meg ducked behind some bushes. She peered through the leaves. An older man stood talking to a short, stocky, younger guy. The older man looked familiar, but the light wasn't good. The two men rushed off toward the carriage house. *Thank God I'm not still in the garage.*

She studied the basement area and noticed blacked out windows. *I bet that's where they're holding Kate.* Meg checked, saw the men still facing the other direction, and scrambled toward the basement door. The knob turned, and she slipped into the gloom.

She saw light coming from a room down the hall and crept toward it. She stared wide-eyed as she looked into a room with a big cage on one end, lights on a bar near the ceiling and chains hanging from the wall. *What is this place?*

Meg sneaked across the room and through another door opening to a long hallway with rooms along one side. The door to the first room opened easily, but she noticed it would be locked from the inside if she allowed it to close. She grabbed a small trashcan by the door and propped it so the door wouldn't close and lock her inside.

Enough light filtered in from the hallway making it easy for Meg to find the light switch. She gasped when she saw a young girl, barely clothed, lying on a cot. *She can't be older than sixteen. Maybe fourteen.*

Meg reached the girl and touched her. Her skin was warm, clammy with beads of sweat along her upper lip. She never opened her eyes. Meg saw an open bottle of pills sitting on the floor. *Where did they get you from? Not the bar.*

She hurried out of the room, careful to close the door again so no one would know she'd been there. Making her way down the hall, she came to another room. She opened the door, and light from the hallway spilled into the darkness. She spotted another girl sitting on a mattress, leaning against the wall. Unable to see clearly, Meg flipped on the light switch.

"Kate!"

Kate didn't open her eyes or even acknowledge Meg's presence. Meg stepped out of her shoe and placed it so the door couldn't close. She hurried toward Kate and knelt in front of her.

"Kate. It's me, Meg." She took the younger girl's head in her hands and hugged her. Kate's eyes were glazed over. "Do you understand me?"

"Meg?" Kate drawled out. Drool ran from her
mouth, and the mattress smelled of urine.

"Kate. Listen. We've got to get you out of
here." She thought of the open bottle of pills in the
other room. Did the guy make it to Kate's room
with the pills yet?

"Mama?" Kate said as her head lolled onto
Meg's shoulder.

Meg felt a tear rolling down her cheek. What
were these people doing? She thought of the cage
and lights in the front room. She realized if the man
came back, she'd be caught and would be of no
help to Kate or that other poor girl.

Somehow, they needed to get away, but she also
needed to stop what was going on in this place.
Whatever they were doing, they were hurting girls.
Meg felt sure Kate and the young girl in the first
room had not been their only victims. These creeps
were involved in sex trafficking.

She heard the basement door open down the
hall and the voices of two men. She couldn't make
out what they were saying, but they were standing
at the door talking.

"Kate," Meg whispered. "Listen to me." Meg
gently slapped the young woman's face. "I've got to
get out of this room, or I'll be no help to you. They
haven't given you a pill yet. When the man comes
in here, don't take the pill. Hold it in your mouth
and spit it out after he leaves. Do you understand?"

"Spith it ouu," Kate slurred.

"Right! Spit it out. I'll be back."

Meg hated leaving Kate in the room, but she had to hide. There was nowhere to hide in the room, and if the door closed, she'd be useless.

Meg grabbed her shoe, eased the door closed, and hurried down the hallway toward the voices.

"I'm calling in some help," Meg heard one of the men say.

"I've got to medicate the other girl," the other voice said, "and I'll come back out and help search."

Meg stepped through a door opposite the room where the young girl lay on a cot. She felt the cold of steel against her back as she pulled the door closed. *This must be a closet for the furnace.*

She looked down and saw a metal louver at the bottom of the door. *It is a furnace and that opening's for ventilation.* She squatted and saw the feet of a man as he unlocked the young girl's door. Meg watched him bend over and place a small piece of wood on the floor so the door wouldn't close and lock.

Easing out of the closet, Meg slipped down the hallway back into the first room. She looked around frantically in search of a place to hide. The cage sat up on a platform, leaving a two-foot opening beneath it. Meg slid under the cage and willed her heart to slow down. She peered out into the room.

On the floor beside the cage, she spotted some discarded clothing and felt a chill run down her back. Beside the cage was a bed along with the chains in the wall she'd spotted earlier. *Is this a torture room?*

On the other side of the room, she noticed a desk and a computer screen. She spotted cameras and a bar hanging from the ceiling with lights. Maybe they made videos in here. Meg heard steps coming down the hallway and slid further back under the platform.

She heard the door open and saw the feet of two men as they stepped into the room. *Two men? Where did the other guy come from? I could have been caught.*

"She's got to be around here, Boss," a male voice said.

Meg sat still as a stone listening intently. *That voice sounds young. Maybe twenties? The boss is the older man.*

"Reggie says he gave her the normal dose of Katamine, so she's probably laying out in the woods somewhere. We found footprints by the carriage house."

"I've got a couple of friends nearby who can help," the younger man said. "You want me to call them?"

The older guy seemed to be considering. "Let's hold off on that, Gage. I don't want anyone else

included in our business if you know what I mean.
Randy and Jeff are on their way. They're probably
bringing Harley with them. That should be enough,
though that only leaves Lucas and Ben with the
other girls."

Meg wished she had something to write on. *The
younger man's name is Gage.*

"We'll find her, Boss."

"We've got to find her," the boss said, "but you
know we can't include her in the auction. She'll
know too much. Reggie has royally screwed up
tonight. Thanks to him, we'll lose some good
money."

"What are you going to do?" Gage asked. "You
said you know who she is."

"We'll get rid of her like we've done before.
You help Reggie search. I'll be out in a minute. I
need to find a phone number."

*Other girls? How many girls did they have, and where
did they keep them?*

Meg watched the older man walk over to the
computer, though all she could see was his legs.
The younger man hurried from the room. She tried
to make herself small and noiseless as she listened
to the sounds of the keyboard clicking. He
continued cursing and pounding the desk.

"I can't believe this," the man muttered. "The
last auction before moving to the warehouse and
now this."

The room grew quiet for a moment, and Meg heard the man's voice from across the room. "Hello, Robert." He must have called someone. "This is Charles."

Charles?

"Listen. I need a favor that will be worth a thousand dollars to you. If you can get it to me in less than five minutes, I'll make it $2,000. This is all off the record, by the way. I need the personal cell number of a real estate guy. He also runs a treasure hunting operation in the Bahamas.

Meg held her breath.

"His name is Jon Davenport."

Chapter Thirteen

Jon leaned on Alberto as they walked toward the exit, Brian right on their heels. He didn't turn his head when he heard Emma's voice.

"Dr. Davenport! You can't leave yet. You've not been discharged."

"I have an emergency," he said over his shoulder and plowed through the doors leading to the parking lot.

When Alberto pulled open the car door, Jon's cell phone buzzed. He looked at the caller ID. Blocked, just like before. He sat down hard on the front seat. "Hello."

He heard a mechanical voice on the other end of the line. "Jon Davenport. I have your wife."

Jon gritted his teeth. "If you hurt Meg, I'll hunt you down and kill you."

The voice on the other end laughed. "So brave, Dr. Davenport. I want ten million dollars, but I want it in Bitcoin. Send me the Bitcoin in time, and she lives. If not, she dies. I want you to print out a receipt of the transfer and take it to a warehouse on the Potomac just north of I-495 at two a.m., Wednesday morning. You'll find your beautiful wife there. I'll send you the address and the numbers you need to make the transfer."

"I want to talk to her."

Jon heard laughter coming through his phone.

"You're in no place to make demands. If you want to see her alive again, be at the warehouse at two a.m. And Dr. Davenport, no cops. I have ears everywhere. If you involve any form of cop, she's dead. Come alone."

The phone went silent. Jon stared at it as a text message came through. It contained an address in Alexandria along with account information for the Bitcoin.

Jon punched the dashboard of Alberto's car which sent a jolt of pain through his head. "Someone has her, Alberto. We've got to find her. Take me to McClanahan's."

Jon stormed through the door of McClanahan's, past the bouncer, and down the hall toward Cyrus Reynolds' office. Alberto intervened and kept the bouncer busy as Jon confronted the owner.

The man stood, and Jon grabbed him by the collar. "I don't know what you've got going on here, but if I don't get my wife back safely, you will regret it."

Brian stepped up and put his hands on Jon's wrists. "Jon, that's not the best way to handle this." He looked at the owner. "Sir, Dr. Davenport's a bit upset. His wife was taken from your bar tonight, and he was attacked outside."

"Have you called the police?" Reynold's asked. "Didn't you say you're FBI?

"No, we're not the FBI, and no police," Jon bit out. "Do you understand? No police."

The owner stepped back and rubbed his hand through his hair.

"Listen," Brian said to the owner. "We don't want to cause you any trouble."

Jon sat down and brought his hands to his face. "I'm sorry, Mr. Reynolds. My wife has been taken, and we've got to find her. If we involve the police, they'll kill her. Will you please help us?"

"I don't know anything about a kidnapping," Reynolds said. "Swear to God."

"I'm sure you don't," Alberto said as he stepped into the office, followed by the bouncer. "The last time we saw Dr. Davenport's wife was when she went into the restroom here. May we go into the restroom?"

"Like Alberto said. Just let us look in the women's restroom. Another girl was taken from here last night, so you've obviously got something going on here that you don't know about."

Reynold's face turned ashen. "I don't know anything about a girl taken."

Alberto stepped toward the desk. "We'd rather keep this quiet for now, Sir. Meg's life is at stake.

We have some resources we can use outside of the police, but we need you to help us keep this quiet."

The owner looked at the bouncer in the doorway. "Louie, keep this to yourself. Got it?"

"Yes, sir, Mr. Reynolds. If that's what you want."

Reynolds nodded, and the bouncer left.

"Come with me," Reynolds said. "You can look around all you want. Please don't make a scene in front of my customers, though. I can't afford to have the place empty out."

They walked into the women's restroom and looked around. Reynolds followed them inside and locked the door behind them.

"No need for someone to come in and wonder what four men are doing in this tiny bathroom," Reynolds said.

Nothing seemed out of place. The restroom was made for one person at a time. It looked like a woman would come inside and lock the door behind her until she was finished. Brian glanced at a tiny white spot on the floor near a large vent cover on the wall.

"Look at this," Brian pointed to the white speck on the floor.

"What is it?" Alberto asked.

"Looks like a small piece of sheetrock," Jon said. He knelt in front of the metal vent cover. Pulling a quarter out of his pocket, he tried to turn the screw holding it to the wall. "Interesting. The screw doesn't turn."

"Let me see," Alberto said as he squatted beside Jon. He pulled on the edge of the vent cover, and it pulled away from the wall a little. Jon held his phone over him with the light turned on. "I can't tell for sure, but it looks like the screw goes into the vent cover instead of through the cover into the wall. It's backward."

Jon turned to where the owner stood just inside the door. "Where's your HVAC system?"

"It's in a closet out back. You get to it from a door outside."

When the men entered the closet from the back alley, they discovered a piece of the wall held in place by small clips. They pulled it away and found a hollow spot in the wall behind the women's restroom. The large vent cover was held in with clips that looked like screws from the other side.

"This isn't really a return," Jon said. "Someone's created a trap door where they can get in and kidnap a woman."

"My guess is someone makes sure a young woman is good and drunk and alerts someone else who's hiding out in here waiting on his next victim."

Brian stepped forward and put his hand on Jon's shoulder. "Let's go to my apartment and figure out what to do. I suggest we also call Jose."

"Jose's on his way," Alberto said. "I called him as soon as I realized Meg was missing."

Chapter Fourteen

Meg couldn't believe what she was hearing. The guy was acting like he had her when in fact, he didn't. Was he just trying to get money out of Jon, or was something else going on? And why wait until two a.m. on Wednesday morning?

She wanted to shout out to Jon and let him know she was okay, but of course, she couldn't. *Ten million dollars in Bitcoin? Don't do it Jon! I'm going to get us out of here.*

He'd said something to that other guy about an auction. That was it. This creep was going to auction off the young girl and Kate. He'd probably do it on the internet. He intended them to be sex slaves. *But that's not going to happen!*

The man's phone conversation ended, and Meg heard him typing on the computer. After a moment, he cursed again, and something hit the wall beside the cage. *Was that his phone? Probably a burner.* She remembered hearing Jon talk about drug runners and terrorists who'd been after them a few years ago using disposable phones that couldn't be traced.

Meg knew she could get Kate out of the house and maybe the young girl, too. What about all the other girls who would be taken in the future? She had to do something to stop this whole operation.

Although Meg wasn't too internet savvy, Kate was. She was getting a degree in information technology. She had to know about it.

Meg imagined Kate lying on the soiled mattress and Gage sticking a pill in her mouth. Hopefully, she spit it out after he left. Meg needed Kate acting at full mental capacity.

As the man stomped toward the basement door, Meg caught a view of his profile. She couldn't place him, but she knew him. Average build. Grey hair. Maybe late fifties or sixty. If she could see his whole face, she might remember.

She waited a couple of minutes to make sure he wasn't coming back. Heart pounding, Meg slid out from under the cage. She hurried down the hall to Kate's room. Kate lay back on the bed, her eyes shut.

"Kate?" Meg whispered and reached out for Kate's hand.

Kate's eyes cracked opened. "Meg?"

"Oh, Kate. Are you okay? Did you spit out the pill?"

Kate smiled and held out her hand showing two pills.

"Great job," Meg said. "Do you feel like sitting up?"

Kate sat up and held her head in her hands. "I don't feel so good."

"I'm sure you don't. You sound better. They've been keeping you drugged. Interesting they use pills instead of a needle."

"I heard them arguing," Kate said. "They used a needle at the bar, and something happened. One guy told them the boss said no needles once they got us out of the bar. Needle marks hurt sale value."

Meg felt sick. They were treating these girls like cattle at an auction. "Kate, these men are running a sex trafficking operation. It seems they have an auction tomorrow night, and by the look of things, they do it online."

"I need to lie down, Meg." Kate said.

"You can't. We don't have long, and we've got work to do."

"What kind of work?"

"I'm not sure. We've got to stop these guys, and we need to expose them for what they're doing. We are in a nice house, and the older guy I saw looks familiar. If we just run, he could get away with all of this, not to mention he'd probably have us hunted down and killed."

"How do you know about an online auction?"

"I heard them mention an auction, and I'm assuming it's online. Do you feel up to walking down the hallway?"

Kate looked at Meg a moment before nodding. Meg helped her get up and held onto her as they walked down the hallway.

"There's another young girl in that room," Meg said as they passed a door. "They've got her drugged, and there's no telling what she's gone through."

Meg led Kate out into what she thought of as the show room and guided her to a chair. Meg pointed out the lights and camera. She shuttered at the thoughts of what had happened in this room and the number of girls paraded through this place.

Kate turned toward the desk. "The computer's on."

Meg looked over and saw the light reflecting off the wall behind the desk. Holding onto the wall, Kate got up and made her way over to the desk. She sat down behind the computer and moved the mouse.

Meg noticed two bottles of pills sitting on the desktop. She picked up one of the bottles and saw it contained small, speckled pills. She read the label on the second bottle: pentobarbital. They had to be some kind of sleeping pills. Maybe one was stronger than the other. She imagined Gage keeping the girls knocked out with one drug and in a mental fog with the other.

"Someone left everything on. We don't need a password to get in."

"Unbelievable," Meg said. "I guess they had no fear of anyone messing with this computer. How would they use the internet to run an auction?"

"They'd use the dark web."

"Dark web?"

"It's a part of the internet that can't be accessed through normal search engines," Kate explained. "You have to use an anonymizing browser called Tor to get to it." Kate moved the mouse around and clicked on a few icons. "There it is. That's exactly what they're doing."

Meg thought for a moment as Kate continued searching on the computer. "We need to expose these creeps so they get caught and can't hurt another girl."

"What do you have in mind?" Kate asked.

"That's the problem. I don't have anything in mind. All I know is we need to make sure the authorities know what's going on here and who's doing it. And we need to get away."

Kate looked around the room. She eyed the cameras directed toward the cage and bed and found the computer program used to control the lights and recording. "Didn't you say this was a really nice house?"

"Yes. It's a regular mansion, but it's been around a long time."

"So, whoever owns it is rich. That would mean he probably has security cameras placed around the house."

"Probably. Whatever you're thinking, we can't get caught. If we hear the slightest noise, you've got to get back into your room and on the bed."

Kate nodded. "I've got an idea."

Chapter Fifteen

"You look like something the cat dragged in."

Jon looked up to see his friend and partner. "Jose! I can't believe you're here already." He stood and wrapped his arms around Jose. Jon's head pounded, but he didn't want to take anything too strong. He needed a clear mind.

"Alberto called me as soon as he figured out Meg was gone. You knew I wouldn't stay home."

"Weren't you with your family in Alabama?"

"Yeah. My father-in-law flew me up here in his Cessna. So, what's going on?"

Alberto and Brian came into the kitchen and joined them. They filled Jose in on the events of the night. Jose pointed out the kidnapper had no need of a receipt of the transaction. He concluded the only reason the kidnapper would have asked for the receipt was he wanted the transaction to go through before Jon left an office with a printer. This delay would give him time to start moving the money from one account to another, making it impossible to trace.

"This guy's plan doesn't make sense," Alberto said. "Why would he give Meg back? It seems a bit risky from his perspective."

"Maybe he discovered Meg's identity and realized he could get some money out of Jon," Brian suggested.

"Possibly," Jose agreed, "but getting Jon personally involved sure seems like a gamble. Think about it. This guy knows he has a woman who may as well be related to the president of the United States. He's got to be nervous about his whole operation being blown to pieces."

"He wants me dead," Jon said as he dropped his head into his hands, "which means Meg may already be dead."

"Brian and I know someone who can get into the city's video surveillance system. Assuming traffic cameras are located near McClanahan's, we should at least be able to discover which direction the kidnappers drove out of town."

Jose rubbed his chin and looked at his watch. "What are the odds we'll find cameras pointing to the alley behind the bar? We'll probably need to find a business with security cameras that may have picked him up."

Brian leaned forward. "Unfortunately, none of the businesses in that area will be open for another five or six hours."

"What about McClanahan's?" Jon asked.
"Surely they've got cameras in the back of their building."

"Already checked," Alberto said. "The one in the back was mysteriously broken, and the owner hasn't gotten it fixed."

"Okay," Jose said. "Let's drive back out to the bar and look around."

"Sounds good," Alberto said. "Let's cross our fingers one of the businesses around McClanahan's has a camera."

"Any other ideas?" Jose asked. The room was silent.

"Jon, you feeling okay?" Alberto finally asked. "I mean is your head feeling all right?"

"Fine," Jon lied. His head pounded relentlessly.

"Jon, you should stay here and take it easy," Jose said. "When we g…"

"Jose," Jon interrupted. "You know I'm not staying here. I can at least help look for surveillance cameras."

Jose closed his eyes. "I had a feeling you'd say that. We need you to be at your best tomorrow."

"I will be. Let's go."

Jon once read about the odds of recovering kidnapped victims and knew their chances weren't good. He could purchase ten million dollars' worth of Bitcoin and move it to the kidnapper's account.

That was the least of his worries; finding Meg alive
was his greatest.

As he grabbed his jacket and headed for the
door, he looked at his watch again. Almost two a.m.
The clock was ticking, and if Meg was still alive,
they'd better hurry and find her.

* * * * *

Meg stood at the basement door on lookout as
Kate rummaged through the closet near the
computer station. She saw Kate pull out a spool of
wire and several other items. Kate eventually
stepped out of the closet with a six-foot ladder.

"What are you doing?" Meg asked.

"I've got a plan, but I'm not sure if it'll work.
Just give me plenty of notice if you see someone
coming."

After another fifteen minutes, several new wires
followed the existing wires that connected the lights
and cameras to the computer. Kate left about a foot
of wire dangling near the cameras before running it
back down to the computer. *What is she up to?*

Meg looked back out the window of the
basement door. "Someone's coming!"

Kate shoved the ladder back into the closet,
followed by the spool of wire.

Meg grabbed Kate's arm and pulled her toward
the hallway. She looked up to the ceiling and

noticed the dangling wires. *No time to fix that.* "Get back to your room and lie down on your mattress. You're supposed to be doped up."

As Kate's door to her room closed, Meg stepped into the closet containing the heating and air unit. She prayed whoever was coming into the basement wouldn't suspect anything or see the wires dangling from the ceiling. She heard the door open to the young girl's room and prayed the man wouldn't hurt her. After a minute, Kate's door opened.

God, please help Kate fool him. Please protect her. Moments later, the door to Kate's room closed, and Meg heard footsteps hurrying down the hall away from the basement door. She realized she had been holding her breath, and she let it out slowly. Her heart was pounding so loudly it was a wonder the guy hadn't heard it.

Meg eased out of her hiding place and opened the door to Kate's room. "You okay?"

"Meg. I've never been so frightened in my life. He had something in his hand. I think it was a knife, maybe. Then, I was afraid he might check my pulse. I remember the other guy doing that earlier. My heart was beating like a drum. If he'd checked, he'd have known I wasn't asleep."

"Oh, Kate. I was praying for you. Was this the older man?"

"I just had my eyes barely open, so I didn't see him very well. I think he was going to hurt me, but his phone buzzed."

"A text?"

"No. He answered it. I think it must have been his wife. He called her, 'Dear.'"

His wife? What a creep! Meg thought about what Kate said. It must have been the older guy who came in for what Reggie called his "sample of the merchandise," but his wife called and interrupted him. From where? Upstairs?

"Kate, I don't know exactly what your plan is, but we've got to get going. I'm assuming the old guy is back upstairs with his wife. Maybe we'll have an hour or two before someone comes back. Maybe."

Kate stood. "If I can have two or three hours and a little luck, that may be all the time I need."

"I don't believe in luck," Meg said as she put her arm around Kate. "I believe in prayer."

Kate grinned. "I don't believe in prayer. So, you pray, and I'll shoot for luck. Hopefully one of us will get what we're aiming for."

Chapter Sixteen

Willing the owner of Capital City Cleaners to answer, Jon looked out the window into the darkness with the phone pressed to his ear. Assuming the camera worked, they'd have a perfect view of any vehicle coming out from behind McClanahan's. The cleaners had a security camera pointing straight at the alley.

It had taken Brian's friend a while to track down the new owner of the cleaners and get his personal cell number. Jon looked at his watch again Five a.m. Shouldn't this guy be up?

"Hello?" came the voice through the phone.

"Mr. Li? This is Jon Davenport. I'm sorry to disturb you so early, but we have an emergency." Jon heard nothing on the other end. "Mr. Li? Are you there?"

As Jon was about to hang up and call again, he heard a different voice. "Hello. This is Chun Li. What emergency?"

"Mr. Li. I'm Jon Davenport. My wife was kidnapped last night at McClanahan's, and we saw your camera pointing toward the alley behind the bar. We hoped we could view video footage from your camera."

"Do you have court order?"

"Mr. Li, it's more complicated than that. If we involve the police, they'll kill my wife."

"I don't know I can trust you, Mr. Davenport. Get a court order."

The phone went dead in Jon's hand. He couldn't believe the guy wasn't willing to help. He turned to Brian. "What time does the cleaners open?"

Brian checked his phone and stared at the screen. "Six."

"Let's go," Jon said. "We can be waiting at the cleaners for Mr. Li to open."

When Jon saw a short, balding, Chinese man walking to the front door, he opened the door to Alberto's car and stepped onto the sidewalk. "Mr. Li. I'm Jon Davenport."

The man reached into his pocket and pulled out a pistol.

"You won't be needing a gun. You can Google my name and verify my identity. I don't intend to harm you. I'm desperate to find my wife."

"If you're desperate, you should involve the police." He turned back to the door with his key in hand.

"Do you have a daughter, Mr. Li? My wife is probably the same age as your daughter."

The man paused with his key in the lock. He faced Jon again. He looked stricken as if Jon had slapped him.

"Do you have a daughter?" Jon asked again and took a few steps toward him. He held out his driver's license for Li to inspect.

The man took the license from Jon's extended hand. He peered at it before handing it back.

"Come in, Mr. Davenport."

"I have three friends with me in the car. They are all former special forces soldiers helping me find my wife. May they come in as well? You can take pictures of us or of our licenses. Whatever will make you feel more comfortable."

Mr. Li looked toward the car and slowly nodded his head. "Yes. They can come in."

Jon motioned with his hand and three car doors opened. Brian, Alberto, and Jose followed Jon and Mr. Li into the cleaners.

"I'm sorry I don't trust people very well," Chun Li said. "Give me a moment, and I'll show you the computer where you can watch the video."

"Thank you so much, Mr. Li," Jon said.

The man turned on lights and disappeared behind racks of clothing. Jon heard several new sounds in the room and assumed the owner flipped a few more switches to machines in the store.

Mr. Li returned to the group and motioned with his hand. "Please call me Chun. My computer is in the back office."

Jon and the others followed through a narrow passageway back to an immaculate little office. Chun sat at a computer and typed in a password.

"I had a daughter," Jon heard Chun almost whisper.

Jon placed his hand on the older man's shoulder. "What happened?"

"Killed. Drug overdose. I blame her boyfriend."

"I'm sorry, Chun," Jon said. "I'm really sorry."

Li stood to his feet and pointed to the chair. "Find your wife."

Jon stepped aside to let Brian sit at the computer. After forwarding through video footage for nearly thirty minutes, Brian hit the pause button.

"There it is," Brian said, staring at the screen.

Everyone leaned forward to see a white, panel van. Brian clicked a button and the van moved forward in slow motion. *Conner's Heating and Air* was painted on the side of the van. He pulled his phone out, took a picture of the computer screen, and dialed a number.

"Dave. It's Brian. I'm sending a picture of a white van. I can't see the tag, but it says Conner's Heating and Air on the side." He listened a moment. "Okay. We'll be waiting. Thanks."

He returned the phone to his pocket. "He'll call back when he knows something."

The men filed out of the little office and found Chun Li at the front counter. The little man did not look up. Jon thought he looked broken.

"We found the van, Chun," Jon said. "Thank you for allowing us to look through the footage." He reached out to shake hands, but Li seemed lost, still unable to meet their gaze.

As they started out the door, Li said again, "Find your wife."

They drove several blocks to a coffee shop called Common Grounds and went inside. They sat in silence drinking coffee. Jon checked his watch every few minutes.

Brian grabbed his phone from the table as it vibrated.

"Put it on speaker," Jon said.

"Hey, Dave. You find it?" Brian asked as he placed the phone on the center of the table. "My friends are listening, too."

"Hey guys," Dave said through the phone. "I followed the white van from McClanahan's and thought I'd lost it. He resurfaced again on M Street and went across the Francis Scott Key bridge."

"That's great, Dave," Brian said. "Any idea which direction from there?"

"That's the tricky part," Dave admitted. "He got on I-66 and went west, but I'm not sure where he went from there. I'm going to keep looking."

"Thanks, Dave," Jon said. "You've helped a lot. Call us if you find out anything else."

They drove back to Brian's apartment, and Alberto spread out a map of Virginia on the kitchen table. He took a red marker and drew a line up the Potomac River. "We can assume she's somewhere west of the Potomac."

Jon dropped his head into his hands. "That narrows it down to about a million square miles."

Chapter Seventeen

Meg plopped down in the chair near the desk and leaned her head against the wall. Her body screamed for sleep, and she felt like someone was poking her head with a sharp object every thirty seconds. She and Kate had somehow made it nearly four hours without anyone coming in to interrupt them.

"Done," Kate leaned back with a grin on her face. "At least I hope I am."

"Will it work?"

"We won't know until we know," Kate said, "but I've done the best I can."

"Kate, you're amazing. Now, we need to stay alive and drug free until the auction."

"So, how do we accomplish that goal?" Kate asked as she stood to her feet and walked toward the basement door.

Meg watched her as the early morning sun began to push back the darkness. "For one thing, we'd better pray no one notices anything missing from upstairs. I still can't believe you sneaked around through the house last night."

Kate turned and flashed her beautiful smile. No wonder she kept getting into trouble with guys.

"I couldn't have done anything last night if you hadn't stood guard for me."

"Maybe, but honestly Kate, if someone had come in when you were upstairs, we'd have been toast."

"They didn't, and we're good."

"We've made it this far, but the next few hours may be the most challenging," Meg admitted.

Meg had spent the night staring out the basement window and standing guard at the bottom of the steps that led up to the main floor of the house. The old guy had been so flustered by his wife's phone call he'd failed to lock the basement door leading to the living area. Kate was able to sneak through the house and make herself at home.

While standing guard, Meg had considered their options. They could run and easily get away. She had no idea how many men were looking for her, but every now and then, she'd notice a flashlight beam shining in the woods around the house. The focus of the search appeared to be the woods behind the house, though it was possible additional men searched around front. Meg didn't think so.

If she and Kate ran, they'd have to carry the younger girl with them. They'd checked on her throughout the night, and she was out cold. Meg figured they could get away, but the crime ring wouldn't be exposed, and the other girls may never be rescued. The creeps would pack up their operation and move. The older guy said something about this being their last auction at his house. He must already have a plan in place.

Kate and Meg's scheme would expose these men, but Meg hadn't quite figured out how to get away and make sure the men were caught red-handed. Kate had offered to remain behind so Meg could run for help, but Meg refused to leave her.

Kate backed away from the door. "Someone's coming."

"You get back on your bed, and I'll hide across the hall. In the meantime, I'll come up with a plan."

They hurried down the hall, and Kate stopped at the door to her room. "Thank you, Meg, for staying with me."

Meg's heart melted. "I believe in you, Kate. We'll get out of this, but in the meantime, you'll need a performance worthy of an Academy Award. I'm praying for you."

As the door to the room closed, Meg slipped into the closet and eased her door closed. As soon as she sat down on the floor, she heard footsteps coming down the hall. She reached her hand out in the darkness to steady herself and felt a metal pipe. She moved her hand from one end of the short pipe to the other. *This could be useful.*

* * * * *

Alberto and Brian had napped a little, but Jon found it impossible to sleep. Jose appeared to be doing something on his laptop for a while before he nodded off to sleep. Jon wasn't sure if he should sleep or not, but his head wasn't throbbing like it had been. Maybe he could function like normal.

He thought back to what they went through the previous summer when Lacy was taken. They'd been frightened, yet Jon had managed to keep his head on right.

This experience was different. Meg was gone and might even be dead. He couldn't just keep sitting here waiting on someone else to find her. He had to do something.

Around eleven o'clock, Brian's phone rang. Brian jerked awake. "Hello." He pressed the speaker phone button.

"Hey, Brian. It's Dave. I've got some news."

"Did you find them?" Jon asked as he moved closer to the phone.

"Yep. At least, I have a better clue as to which direction they went. I've studied every bit of video footage from every traffic camera imaginable."

"Dave," Jon interrupted, "where are they?"

"They got on I-66 but ended up coming back to George Washington Parkway and going north. I'm thinking the guy missed the turn or was trying to throw someone off his trail. Who knows?"

Jon walked over to the table where the map was still lying, He slid his finger across the Francis Scott Key bridge coming across the Potomac River and allowed his eyes to drift north on George Washington Parkway.

"It seems if he were going to McLean or Tysons, he would have taken I-66," Jon said. "There aren't a lot of options along the Parkway. I think we can move the bottom of our circle to Langley and go north toward Great Falls, and…what is that? Shady Oak? Or even Potomac Falls."

Alberto and Brian moved closer and stared at the map. Brian held the phone in his hand.

"Anything else, Dave?" Brian asked.

"I think that's it, for now. I'll keep studying the area, but I don't think I'm going to find anything else. Sorry."

"You've done great. Thanks."

Brian hung up and leaned over the map.

Jon settled his laptop on the table and punched a few keys. "Guys, I think Dave is right, except I don't think he went as far north as Potomac Falls. If he was going there, he would have taken I-66. That leaves us the vicinity of Great Falls."

"Makes sense," Alberto agreed.

"I think we should find a hotel in Great Falls and set up our base there," Brian said.

Jose tapped a few more keys. "Here's a Homewood Suites in Reston. That's the closest hotel we'll get to Great Falls."

"Get us a suite," Jon said. He grabbed his jacket. "Let's go, guys."

Chapter Eighteen

Meg heard men shuffling in and out of the basement for a while, but no one seemed to go into Kate's room. *Thank you, Lord!* It seemed they were moving things around, and Meg felt her heart drop at the thought of them discovering the additions Kate made to their light bar during the night.

She heard conversations from several voices. *Definitely more than two men in there.* She couldn't make out everything but could tell they were talking about bringing in the other girls. *When is this auction?*

Meg peered at her watch in the darkness of the closet and saw it was almost one o'clock. She knew Jon would be sick with worry and doing everything he could to find her. She had to expose these criminals and somehow get herself and the other girls to safety.

Her eyelids were heavy as if thick chains were pulling them closed, but she rubbed her eyes and pinched herself. She couldn't fall asleep. She hadn't come up with a solid plan of escape, and she had no idea how much more time she had. The closet was pitch black except for a little light seeping in through the metal vent in the door.

She felt warm as memories of meeting Jon on Nassau several years ago filled her mind. Images of scuba diving with him and searching for treasure floated through her thoughts. She could almost feel his arms around her, the heat from his body warming her, as they hid in the cave on Conception Island.

Meg gave herself to his embrace. She felt safe, secure, and enveloped in his love.

Meg jerked awake at the screaming from across the hall. *Kate?* She grabbed the metal pipe lying on the floor and stepped out of the closet.

She jerked open the door and rushed toward the young man reaching for Kate. With all her might, she swung the pipe at his head. Because he was bent over, his shoulders took the brunt of the blow. He fell to his knee, cursing, but in a flash, he shoved off the floor and spun around to face Meg.

She swung the pipe a second time, but he blocked it and reached for her throat. Adrenaline pumped through her body, and her self-defense training made her moves reflexive. Meg shoved her hands between his arms and out, which forced his hands off her throat. Her knee came up hard, sending a paralyzing blow. The man doubled over.

"Run, Kate!"

Meg turned and ran from the room, right into the arms of an older man. She looked into his face and froze. *Senator Charles Fields?*

Slamming the door in Kate's face, the senator pinned Meg's arms to her side. She felt his strength squeezing her as she struggled against him.

Another man came toward her, and she used the leverage of the senator's grip to kick the man in the face. He fell back in a daze.

The senator breathed on her neck as he moved his mouth to her ear. She dropped her head forward and came back hard on his nose. She heard a horrible crack and blood sprayed onto her shoulder. The senator only squeezed harder.

He wrestled her into the control room where Meg saw the cage out of the corner of her eye. He threw her toward the wall, and she fell onto the bed. As she bounced face down onto the bed, she heard the unmistakable sound of Senator Fields chambering a round into a gun.

Meg felt around for something under the bed, anything, that could be a weapon. Charles took two strides toward the bed and grabbed her by the hair. He put his knee into her back and snatched her head up. She felt the cold steel of the gun against the side of her temple.

She was going to die. But she felt no fear, only peace. If it was her time to meet God, she welcomed it.

Her hand closed around something small and rectangular. As the senator's fist connected with her cheek, which sent her body toward the wall, she clutched the object. Even as her world tilted, and blood dripped from her mouth, she squeezed the object with all her strength.

Meg opened her eyes and could see through the crack between the bed and the wall. She was holding a phone—the cheap, flip phone Charles had thrown earlier. She opened it with one hand, and the light came on. Pressing a button, she saw two recent calls. She recognized Jon's number and pressed it.

The senator jerked her out of the bed, and Meg finally lost her grip on the phone. He slammed her against the wall. Meg felt the wind knocked out of her as she crumpled to the floor. He pulled her up and shook her.

His nose bled profusely as he snarled at her. He looked like a rabid dog. He cursed and slapped her face again.

Her nose began to bleed, and the left side of her face felt numb. Charles pulled chains that hung from the wall. Meg recognized the old-fashioned manacle. He clamped it around her wrists and pressed his body against hers.

She spit on him. He cursed again and punched her stomach. She doubled over and vomited on his legs.

Charles screamed and grabbed her throat. He forced her head against the wall and growled at her.

"You've caused me a lot of trouble, Meg Davenport. You're dead."

Meg raised her knee, but he twisted out of the way. He wrapped his arms around both her legs.

"Harley," Charles yelled.

A younger man stood across the room where he'd been watching the show.

"Chain her feet."

Harley grabbed two additional chains that connected to the floor, and he clamped them around her ankles. The short chains held her fast. Meg tried to fight, but she was quickly losing strength.

Charles stood, grabbed her chin with one hand, and pressed her body against the wall. He glared into her eyes with more rage than Meg had ever seen. His breath smelled like a septic tank, and her own vomit made the room putrid.

"We're going to let you watch our parade of talent," Charles sneered, "and then we're going to let our clients watch while my men show them what we do with troublemakers. If you survive their fun, you won't survive mine."

Chapter Nineteen

Jon grabbed his phone on the first ring. He read the screen and saw the caller had his ID blocked, like the last time. "Hello."

No one said anything on the other end, but Jon heard a scuffle. He heard a slap and the groan of a woman. "Meg!" Jon felt as if his heart stopped.

He heard a man scream, or something more like a growl. Someone was fighting. He heard the man yell again, "You've caused me a lot of trouble, Meg Davenport. You're dead."

Jose stepped beside him. "Give me the phone, Jon. We can track this."

"I'm calling Dave," Brian said as he pulled his phone out of his pocket.

Jon stood. "He's beating her!" he exclaimed. "We've got to find her."

Jose hung up Jon's phone. "Ask Dave what the two numbers are I need to dial to get the number that just called Jon's phone. I can't remember them."

Brian spoke into his phone and turned to Jose. "Star sixty-nine."

Jose read the number on Jon's screen off to
Brian but said it loud enough so Dave could hear it
on the other end. Brian talked to Dave for a
moment before disconnecting.

"He's got someone who can ping that number,"
Brian said. "He said we should get in the car and be
ready to go."

"I'll kill him," Jon breathed through his teeth.

"Jon, you can't lose your head," Jose said.
"We'll get her."

They raced to the car in the parking lot and
started it up. When Brian's phone rang, he put it on
speaker phone.

"Head toward Shady Oak. We're working on a
triangulation."

Alberto tapped his phone, and the screen lit up
with directions to the little community of Shady
Oak. He put the car in gear and sped out of the
parking lot.

"Brian," Dave's voice came out of the phone,
"you still there?"

"Yes. What do you have?"

Brian said the name of a street with two
possible locations. He mentioned a third they
should also consider. "We're not able to get an
exact location, but this one's pretty close. I think it's
the first one. There are not a lot of houses on that
street."

In less than fifteen minutes, Alberto turned left onto the street Dave had mentioned and eased the car down the road. Brian's phone rang again.

"Guys, you're not going to believe this. That first address belongs to the estate of Senator Charles Field's mother. It's tied up in probate, so I'm not sure if the senator lives there or not."

Alberto killed the engine a little before the driveway leading to the old mansion. "Make sure your phones are on vibrate." Each man checked his phone as they ran toward a row of shrubs shielding the house from the road.

Jon saw what looked like three vans parked on the drive around the back of the house.

"This has to be it," Jon said as he felt his phone vibrate.

He looked at the caller ID and pulled his phone to his ear. "Randall?"

"Jon, I just got a message from Anthony Wiley, the FBI director. Where's Meg?"

Jon felt sick. Should he tell his father-in-law what was going on? "What do you mean, Randall?"

"Someone alerted Anthony of a live broadcast on Facebook. It's coming from Kate's homepage. Jon, it looks like a sex trafficking ring, and the woman chained to the wall looks like Meg."

"Randall, I think I'm at the place where this is being done. I'm here with Jose and couple of our friends."

"Jon. Don't go in. Give me the address, and I'll have police there in a few minutes."

Jon saw Jose look around the bushes toward the house and motion for them to follow.

"Randall, I'm going in, but I'll give you the address." While running toward the house, Jon gave the president the address and thrust his phone in his pocket.

Jose burst through the basement door and instantly took a bullet in his side. He shoved the gun out of the way and drove the palm of his hand into the nose of the shooter.

Jon followed and saw Senator Fields run across the room to a hallway leading away from the door. A man wearing a mask held a woman who didn't appear to be lucid. They stood in the center of an area lit with high-powered lights. Jon scanned the room and saw Meg on the other side, collapsed on the floor. Her arms were outstretched and chained to the wall.

As he ran across the room toward Meg, a man raised a pistol in his direction, but Jon tackled him and pummeled the guy's face with his fists. Several shots reverberated in the room and the sound of fighting echoed in the cavernous space.

Jon pulled Meg into his arms. Her head drooped and blood dripped from her nose.

Lifting her head, she looked into his eyes. "I knew you'd come."

In a matter of minutes, two men lay lifeless on the floor and three more writhed in pain with broken limbs.

Jon heard sirens in the distance as he called out for someone to find a key to the manacles. "Someone get the senator!" A car raced out of the driveway, and Jon knew Charles Fields was gone.

Alberto produced a key, and as soon as Jon removed the chains from Meg's wrist and ankles, she fell into his arms.

"Call an ambulance, Brian," Jon ordered. "Jose, are you okay?"

"It's not bad," Jose said. "I'll be fine."

"Where's Kate?" Meg asked barely above a whisper.

Jon saw Brian and Alberto helping women sit down in the chairs by the wall. They all appeared to be drugged. He looked up and noticed Kate and a younger girl inside a large cage. Kate leaned against the bars of the cage with her eyes closed.

"Alberto," Jon said. "Check the girls in the cage."

Alberto fished a key out of the pocket of the guy who shot Jose and unlocked the cage. Reaching inside, he pulled a young girl out who looked to be about fourteen years old. He handed her to Brian and picked up Kate.

"This is your niece?" Alberto asked. "She's breathing but on something."

"That's her," Jon said. "Not exactly my niece, but…"

Police ran into the basement with weapons drawn. "No one move," one of them barked out. "Jon Davenport?"

"I'm here," Jon said, raising his hand. "These three men are with me."

The police holstered their weapons and began to take charge of each of the traffickers who were still alive.

"Senator Charles Fields is involved in this, too," Jon said.

"We know," an officer said. "The video was blasted on Facebook, and he was front and center. There's no denying it."

Jon marveled. How had all of this gotten onto Facebook?

Paramedics rushed into the room, and Jon waved them over to take care of Meg. "Jose's also been shot."

"We've got her from here, sir," one of the paramedics said as another tended to Jose's wound. "We'll be transporting her to the hospital."

"May I ride with you?"

"I'm sorry. You'll have to follow in your own vehicle."

"Come on, Jon," Alberto said. "I'll take you. They don't need me here anymore."

Jon turned toward the paramedic checking Meg's injuries. "What about Kate?" he motioned toward the young woman leaning against the wall, "and Jose?"

"They'll be transported as well."

"Brian," Jon said, "will you watch over Kate? I'm going to the hospital."

Chapter Twenty

On Friday morning, two nurses rolled Meg and Kate out the hospital door as Jon pulled up and jumped out of the car. Looking at Meg sitting in the wheelchair, he felt a lump form in his throat. He knew this chapter could have had a very different ending.

He opened the car door and helped Meg onto the seat. The morning sun highlighted her swollen and bruised face.

"I'm fine, Honey," Meg said. "Really. I can get into the car. They should have let me go home yesterday."

"You know they needed to watch over you to make sure everything was okay," Jon said. "Nothing wrong with being cautious."

"You may want to milk this for a while," one of the nurses said with a wink. "Mr. Davenport, she'll probably need her feet rubbed as soon as she gets home."

"And her hair washed," the other one added.

Jon smiled at them. "I can handle that."

Kate got out of the wheelchair and walked to the back door of the car. She turned to the nurses. "All of you have been so wonderful. Thank you."

"It's not every day we get to take care of celebrities," one nurse said.

"We're nobodies," Jon said. "And remember you all agreed you never saw us, right?"

The first nurse stepped forward. "I suppose you're fortunate we voted for President Johnson and plan to do so again. Our lips are sealed."

The streets of Washington, DC were quiet as many had left the city for the long holiday weekend. Jon glanced at Meg and reached out to hold her hand. He wanted to get her home and take care of her, but they had to spend the weekend with their family first. Christmas at the White House hadn't turned out quite like they'd expected.

"You are a hero," Jon said. He looked in the rearview mirror. "Both of you."

"I guess I'm glad no one will ever know about it," Kate said, "though it may have helped me get a job one of these days."

Jon laughed. "I don't think you'll have any trouble getting a job. Using Senator Fields' security cameras to put him on Facebook was brilliant."

Kate beamed, but Jon noticed a tear trickle down her cheek. "Meg's the real hero. She saved my life. This whole ordeal has given me a lot to think about."

"I'm proud of you both," Jon said.

"What about Jose?" Meg asked.

"He's going to be fine. He'll be flying back to be with Ann in Alabama later this afternoon," Jon said. "She wanted to come up, but he insisted she stay with her family. I told him I'd come back and get him when he was discharged."

Jon pulled into the entrance of the White House and followed the driveway to the West Wing. He smiled as he saw Ryan's familiar face. Ryan opened the door for Meg as Jon hurried around the car.

"Good morning, Ryan," Jon said.

"Good morning, Dr. Davenport. Congratulations. I understand you've managed to keep your names out of the media, but all of us around here are impressed."

"Thank you, Ryan. We never would have figured it out without your help. Now, we're hoping to have a boring holiday with our family."

Ryan held the door as everyone entered the long colonnade. "You've earned it. Merry Christmas."

"Merry Christmas," Jon said.

The elevator door opened to the second floor living quarters, and Jennifer rushed up to Kate. Jon heard more voices down the hallway.

Jennifer wrapped her arms around her daughter. "Oh, Sweetheart. I'm so sorry I didn't make it to the hospital this morning. You left earlier than I thought you would. I was getting ready to come, and next thing I knew, Jon was on the phone telling me he'd bring you."

"It's fine, Mom. No big deal. Where's Dad?"

"He'll be back after a while. You know he's been working on a big case and had to complete a deposition this morning. He should be back in time for dinner."

Jon noticed Kate's disappointment. "Come on, Kate. Why don't you and Meg come into the living room and tell everyone your story. I hear Lacy's voice, and I'm sure Kerrick and Judy must be in there, too."

"Mommy!" Carla ran down the hallway into Meg's arms.

"Oh, Baby. I am so happy to see you."

Carla placed her finger on Meg's cheek. "Boo boo?"

"Yes, Sweetie. Mommy has a boo boo."

Carla kissed Meg's cheek. Jon picked up his little girl, and they joined the rest of their family. A beautifully decorated Christmas tree sat in one corner of the room with gifts covering the floor underneath.

He hugged Lacy and shook Kerrick's hand. "You missed all the excitement."

Lacy hugged Meg. "We heard. I'm so glad you're all okay."

"Lacy and Kerrick," Jon said, "This is Kate, and I'm sure you've already met Jennifer."

Lacy hugged Kate. "It's so good to meet you, Kate, and I'm glad you're all right."

"I wouldn't be if it weren't for Jon and Meg. Meg saved my life."

"I also heard it's because of you Senator Fields will be serving time rather than our country," Lacy said. "You rock. Putting them on Facebook! What a great idea."

Randall and Gina walked into the room and hugged everyone.

"Welcome home, Randall," Jon said as the two sat down. Everyone else found a seat.

"Thank you, Jon. It was a productive week, but it seems I missed a lot while I was gone. Meg and Kate, we all want to hear the whole story."

"First," Kate said, "I want to say I'm sorry. All this happened because of me being stupid. I put Meg in danger and Jon. You two saved my life. I've got a lot to be grateful for and a lot to think about."

Reaching over to hold Kate's hand, Meg said, "We all do."

"We all love you, Kate," Gina said as she got up and hugged her granddaughter. "We all have experiences we wish we could have avoided, but it's amazing how God uses those experiences for our good if we let Him."

Kate dropped her gaze. Jon couldn't tell if she was embarrassed or simply pondering what Gina said.

Breaking the awkwardness, Meg said, "I wish you all could have seen Kate. She took over and put together a plan that ultimately caught the senator red-handed."

Meg and Kate shared their story. Jon's heart was full and his eyes wet with unshed tears as the details of their experiences unfolded. He added his perspective from time to time and felt blessed beyond measure.

"I looked up," Meg finally concluded, "and Jon was there. I knew he'd come."

"They took us to the hospital," Kate continued, "and you know the rest of the story."

"It may take a week or two for my face to look okay," Meg said, "but I'm grateful. It could have been worse. And of course, Jon's head." She reached over to touch the back of his head but dropped her hand to his shoulder.

"Let's just say it's a good thing I'm hardheaded," Jon said. He leaned over and kissed Meg's cheek. "We're all grateful."

"You two saved all of those women's lives." Lacy said. "It's kind of a shame they'll never know who helped them. Why did you want to keep your name out of the papers?"

Jon looked at Randall. "We felt like it would be best if Randall weren't connected to bringing down one of his fiercest enemies, Senator Fields. With Randall's re-election campaign in full force, I figured he didn't need that kind of press."

"Charles has been trying to ruin me for a long time," Randall said. "Thank you for thinking of that Jon. I'm sure the media would have gotten a lot of mileage out of this story."

"I'm glad you were able to keep Meg and Kate's names out of the story for other reasons, too," Jon said. "If that had gotten out, we could kiss a quiet Christmas goodbye."

Jon winked at Meg and her lips turned up in a smile. Her bruised face broke his heart. She was supposed to be a Christmas guest, but she'd become a Christmas captive. He planned to do everything possible to turn this Christmas vacation around.

"I'm going to pick up Jose in a while and see him off at the airport," Jon continued. "Then, I'd like to come back and enjoy the next few days as if none of this happened."

"I like the sound of that," Meg said. "A quiet Christmas at the White House. After that, I'd like to go home and have at least another ten years of quiet before more craziness starts up."

"Look out!" Kerrick yelled as he jumped to his feet. He managed to grab the Christmas tree just before it toppled over onto Carla. Ornaments crashed to the floor. Her little hands still gripped the branches of the tree.

After a moment of silence, everyone burst into laughter.

"Honey," Gina said, "maybe we can make it through a quiet Christmas, but I'm afraid your next ten years are going to be anything but quiet."

Note from the Author

Thank you for reading *Christmas Captive*. I hope you enjoyed reading it as much as I enjoyed writing it. Though I wrote this as a stand-alone novella, I'm sure you can tell it fits neatly into a series I began writing a few years ago called the *Davenport Series*.

You probably saw an offer for a gift I'm offering. It's a novella that shares a story of Jon and Meg's relationship when Meg was an awkward middle-schooler and Jon was a popular high school jock. If you haven't downloaded it yet, you can get it on my website (https://judahknight.com/free-gift/). If you're interested in learning about the other six books in the Davenport Series, check out the following pages.

Would you be so kind as to share a review of this book? If you enjoyed *Christmas Captive*, would you visit your retailer and write a brief review? Your opinion will be so valuable in helping others as they look for their next clean, romantic, suspense book to read.

I'd love to hear from you, so feel free to visit my website and drop me a note from the contact page. Share with me your thoughts about my books as well as some of the other books in this genre you've enjoyed the most.

Thanks again for taking the time to read *Christmas Captive*. I hope you'll tell someone else about the book, and I'll see you in the next adventure.

Judah Knight

The Davenport Series

Book 1: The Long Way Home

He had a boat. She needed a ride. A simple lift turned into the adventure of a lifetime. Jon Davenport and Meg Freeman had a chance encounter in Nassau that would change their lives and destinies. Scuba diving, treasure hunting, action, romance, and suspense! The Davenport series is written for adults, but it's safe for the whole family.

Book 2: Hope for Tomorrow

Our tomorrows can be different than our yesterdays! Jon Davenport invited Meg Freeman, along with her friend Ann, to join him in searching for sunken treasure in the Bahamas. Though Meg searched for gold, the treasure she found was far more valuable.

Visit judahknight.com for more information.

Book 3: Finding My Way

Bitterness. Betrayal. Brokenness. Can the search for ancient gold help her find lasting treasure? Meet the Davenport's niece, Lacy Henderson, as she joins the adventure in the Bahamas, along with summer intern, Kerrick Daniels.

Book 4: Ready to Love Again

She had given up on love until…
Lacy Henderson went to the Bahamas to help her aunt and uncle in a boys' program, but she seems to be the one who had the greatest summer of all.

Book 5: Love Waits

The Dream of a Lifetime…or a nightmare in disguise? Though the summer is completed, Lacy and Kerrick's relationship is far from over. The two join the Davenports on a search for lost treasure that takes them from the Bahamas to Mexico. Lacy learns that love hurts, but also, love waits.

Book 6: No Greater Love

True love costs everything. The Davenports, along with Lacy, Kerrick, Jose, and Ann return to Mexico with dreams of finding ancient treasure and a lost Mesoamerican city. The clues are promising, but the expedition gets diverted. A friend has gotten caught up in the Mexican Cartel, and the Davenports must help him. Their search sends them on a perilous journey that ends in pain, hope, loss, and love. What's next when hope is not a possibility?

Prequel: A Girl Can Always Hope

In *The Long Way Home*, we learn that the two main characters knew one another as teenagers, and Margaret Robertson (Meg Freeman in *The Long Way Home*) had a crush on her brother's best friend, Jon Davenport. Read the fun short story of one awkward middle schooler's attempt to capture the impossible catch. This book is available as a gift on the author's website: judahknight.com.

For more information on any of our books, visit greentreepublishers.com.

www.ingramcontent.com/pod-product-compliance
Lightning Source LLC
Chambersburg PA
CBHW061246170626
46809CB00007B/2872